Imara's life is going according to her plans. She has her boyfriend, her kitten, and is about to earn her degree in Magecraft and graduate. Once she has that degree, she has the right to request an application for a commercial magic license. It is the goal she has been working toward all along.

A shadow begins to haunt her during the day and stalk her when she is away from the college. She doesn't know what it wants, but it follows her with a purpose she can't fathom until she finds the identity of her stalker.

By the time she learns that it is Mr. E the stalker is after and not her, the trap has already closed.

JAN - - 2023

D1570372

Spell Crafting 501
Copyright © 2018 by Viola Grace
ISBN: 978-1-987969-49-8
©Cover art by Angela Waters

Spell Crafting 501
Published by Viola Grace

Look for me online at violagrace.com, Amazon, Sea to Sky Books, Smashwords, Kobo, B&N and other ebook sellers.

Spell Crafting 501
The Hellkitten Chronicles

By

Viola Grace

Chapter One

Smara took inventory of the magical-items cupboard for the fifth time. She worked to get every herb, powder, and weird liquid committed to memory.

No Mage has all their herbs committed to memory. You are going to burn your nose out. Mr. E was sitting on the counter amid the bottles and cleaning his paws. It wouldn't be so odd, but he was wiping them with a tiny hanky that she didn't remember giving to him.

She put the bottles carefully back in the cupboard. "My nose is fine. I just want to be careful with my studies. I have to do half the work in class, so it is going to be difficult to do things with someone watching."

Yes. I can imagine. You do your best work with the dead. Why are you taking this course again?

Imara looked over at him. "Short time, high credit."

Ah. Right. I saw the application for commercial magic in your room. Everything is filled out but the date of application.

She made a face as she kept loading the cupboard. "Sue me for being positive. I am hoping that I don't have to tear it up and go back to the college board for a full course load next semester."

I don't want to stay around here any longer than I need to. What can I do to help?

"Well, I have two days before the classes start, and each evening, I have tours of the local mage repositories with mage guides and members of the XIA. I hope I can tell them apart." She smiled slightly. "They are delighted to have access to the spectres via their cooperation with the Mage Guild or the Death Keeper's guild."

The mage guides? They are getting really advanced. He smirked. *You do have much more of an affinity with the other Death Keepers than with mages. Those who work with the dead are rather easygoing.*

Imara closed the glass door and latched it. "That is because we are the conversational superstars of the night."

To be fair, you are competing with the dead.

"I am not competing with the dead; I am competing with the sentient magic of the dead. There is a vast difference." She wrinkled her nose and picked him up, tucking him up on her shoulder and walking down the hall toward the common space.

Reegar was sitting and reading a tome that he had probably memorized, and Bara was sitting on the couch with her feet up, embroidering a sash.

Imara went to the kitchen and got a cup of coffee.

Bara called out, "Another late night coming up?"

Imara walked out of the kitchen and over to the loveseat that she called her own. "Yeah."

Bara gave her a quirked look. "Is it worth it?"

Imara sipped at her coffee and then replied, "It is. I am introducing people to a skill set and resource that has dwindled dramatically. Nine families that I have dealt with have now put spectres in their wills. It benefits us and their heirs."

"Don't you feel weird selling services to the dead?"

Imara sighed. "I am not selling anything. I just demonstrate how useful it would be if their children's and grand-children's essences remain available for consultation."

Bara blinked. "I don't see the purpose."

Imara leaned back. "I am primarily called on when there is an unresolved legal matter or an event regarding a property. Not everyone passes with a copy of their will in their hands, but the settings for a spectre can kick in automatically, and their mind can be consulted the next day."

Bara whistled. "That makes a lot of sense."

"Thank you. The repositories set the spectre stones in a larger obelisk, and that provides the power of projection for the consciousness."

Bara grinned. "Now I don't have to take a tour."

Imara snorted. "You never had to. It

is just like what I did for Reegar. He is powered up and able to interact as if he were still living."

"Aside from being confined to the hall."

Imara wrinkled her nose. "There are options for that, but the hall is acting as the obelisk. There are so many objects of power here that they are making his projection easy. I healed his fading spectre, and he is doing the rest."

Reegar snorted from his corner. "I can hear you, you know."

Bara laughed. "We know. It is definitely nice to actually see you now and not just feel you lurking about."

Reegar looked up with a smile on his dapper features. "I just wanted you to know that I was here and I was paying attention. No frolicking or odd behaviour in my home."

Bara grinned and returned her attention to her embroidery. "I know, and I had no intention of doing anything else other than studying."

Imara chuckled. "With a mind like yours, I am amazed that you aren't entering the Mage Guild's research and development department."

"Organized research isn't for me. I much prefer to gain skill after skill and simply hoard them." Bara looked up and winked.

"I respect your choice and enjoy your talents." She finished her coffee and checked the time.

Reegar flicked a look at her. "Are you going to wait for Argus?"

"No, he is picking me up for tomorrow's tour. Tonight, it is the mage guides again. Different group and different memorial garden." She got to her feet.

Bara asked, "What is the difference between a repository and a memorial garden?"

Imara smirked and headed for her

7

room, yelling out, "The tax base."

She heard the snort as she walked up the stairs to her room, one hand absently holding on to Mr. E. It was time to get changed into her robes and get into her car for the hour's drive to the small town near Redbird City. The highway was the easiest part of that night's excursion. The mage guides she was meeting with were all under the age of ten. They were confident enough to ask questions and young enough to not have a grasp of the adult world. It made conversations with the spectres a little wearing. Keeping spectres from using foul language was sometimes an uphill battle.

Imara settled her robes on and around Mr. E, and she smiled. She loved her job.

After an hour of driving with the radio blasting and Mr. E singing along with the rock ballads that she found, she turned off the noise and pulled into the parking lot outside of the Redbird City Garden of Spectral Retirement. Imara kept herself from smiling as she got out of her car, and Mr. E perched on her shoulder. That was a very grand way of saying *this way to talking rocks.*

Imara hadn't been to this facility before, so she made sure that Mr. E was tucked in before she walked to the welcome building.

The first thing she saw was the flicker of a screen in the back corner of the room, and she investigated. The staffer was sitting in the corner and sleeping. Her chest was rising and falling slowly, so it was almost difficult deciding to wake her.

Let me do it. Mr. E's words were loud in her head.

Imara shrugged and let him down, holding her hand out so he could simply walk down her arm. He hopped lightly to the desk and sat in front of the flickering screen.

She was about to ask what he was going to do when he opened his little mouth and yowled loud enough to make the lights flicker.

The woman screamed, tilted back, and thudded to the ground before she scrambled to her feet with her hair wild and her eyes white in her dark features.

"What the hell was that?"

Mr. E sat licking his paws like a normal kitten. Only Imara could hear his inner guffaws.

"My familiar wished to wake you, miss. I am Master Imara. I will be leading the tour tonight."

The woman blinked. "That's tonight?"

"It is. I have confirmed with the mage guides. They will be here in half an hour. Just tell me which zones would have the most friendly spectres, please." Imara smiled.

"Uh... I don't really know." The woman straightened the chair and sat down. "I am just keeping the chair warm. The actual Death Keeper went to a concert in town and told me that nothing was happening tonight."

Imara winced. "Right. I am going to go for a quick tour. If the mage guides arrive, stand with your back straight, fold your hands in front of you like this."

She demonstrated, and the woman stood and mimicked her.

"Excellent. Tell them that Master Imara will be here shortly and show them the video in the visitor's centre. It is already primed for the visit."

The woman looked over, and she frowned. "That ass."

Imara grinned. "Yeah, he knew we were coming. What is your name, by the way?"

"Connie. Thanks for being cool with this."

Imara winked. "Make sure that he gives you the share of the four hundred dollars that the guild is paying him for the tour."

Connie stared at her, and something strange happened. A flicker of magic ran across her skin. Imara blinked several times as the woman's skin went granulated and then smoothed back into the medium brown of her normal tone.

Imara paused and then said, "I am just going to check the gardens, looking for something that won't curse in front of the kids."

Connie blinked. "They do that?"

"They have all the bad and good habits of their human lives, without the soul. It can make for some exciting conversations."

Imara held her hand out, and Mr. E made a phenomenal leap from the desk to her bicep, and then, he curled around her neck once again.

Connie looked like she didn't know what to do, so she turned off her screen and was straightening items in the entry room when Imara went through the warded doorway and into the gardens.

She let a short wave of spectral energy out and walked toward the bank of elder stones that she could feel in the distance.

Imara walked along for a few minutes and found the spot that had a sign indicating that it was *The Garden of Repose.*

She walked into the shadowed darkness, and she spoke, "Is there anyone here who wants to speak to a group of mage guides? I will be bringing the girls this way in a few minutes if you are willing to be polite and informative."

A few flickers of energy formed into spectres, so she powered them up.

"What are you, miss?"

The woman was wearing ancient robes, and her eyes were focusing on

Imara.

"I am a Death Keeper. I just happen to be very good at my job."

The woman smiled slightly. "I will speak to your young ladies."

"Who are you, Madam?"

"Magus Elder Reetha Nakura. I passed over three hundred years ago."

"I am Master Imara Mirrin. Death Keeper and tour guide when necessary. I can also rejuvenate spectres. I have an affinity for the dead."

The woman bowed. "I will await your tour eagerly. How long will I remain visible to the living?"

"How long do you wish to be? I can make you transparent for the time being and then introduce the girls to you as you solidify."

The elder quirked her lips. "That sounds like more fun than I have had in decades."

"How many others are here?" Imara

could feel nine, but they were all very faint.

"Seven. All masters like myself."

Imara kept her face emotionless. "Excellent. I look forward to bringing them here."

She withdrew the power she had donated to the elder and the others. She bowed to the empty space, and she walked out.

She kept her shiver of dread until she was away from their sphere of influence.

"Well, the kids don't need that."

Mr. E shivered a little. "Do you think she recognized me?"

"Someone in there did. There were nine signatures aside from the elder. She wanted me to bring them all out, and that means there were two people in there she didn't want me to know about. I am going to a weak target, not a faded one."

She hunted around and found something suitable. An instructional mage who had died one hundred forty years ago, but she was the last of her line. No one visited. She was happy for the company and the promise of letting her magic drain into silence.

With her willing participant in the demonstration charged and waiting, Imara returned to the welcome centre. It was time to lecture the little ones.

Chapter Two

$\mathcal{I}$nstead of little ones, a group of teen-agers was there with a harried-looking guide leader and two adult women. Imara grinned. "Benny!"

Benny Ganger came forward and shook Imara's hand. "When I heard who was doing the tour, I had to come. This is my best buddy, Freddy. Freddy, this is Imara, the Death Keeper."

Freddy extended her hand, and when Imara took it, she read generations of suffering and torment embodied in the soul of the woman.

Mr. E moved in a blur and sniffed at Freddy's hand. Instead of growling at the taste of the demon magic, he rubbed

17

his head against her knuckles while perching on Imara's wrist.

Hellhound. There was pity in his voice.

Don't you despise magic from the demon zone? she asked him softly.

No, I despise demons and those who traffic with them. Hellhounds are mages bound to draw on the demon zone energy at the will of other mages. She's a slave.

Imara looked at Freddy's face, but the other woman was exclaiming how cute Mr. E was.

"He's adorable!"

Imara released Freddy's hand and scooped up her familiar. "He really is. Would you like to hold him?"

Freddy nearly snatched him away and proceeded to murmur to him and cuddle him.

Imara ignored the black thoughts coming her way, and she turned to Benny. "So, you are just here for the tour?"

"Yes, and to keep these ladies on track." Benny jerked her head at the teens who were paying more attention to them than the video screen.

"Well, in that case, we should start the show." She beckoned, Mr. E squirmed free from Freddy's kisses, and was back on her shoulder in a bound.

Imara stepped toward the Guide Master, and she introduced herself to Sandy Dale. Once that was done, she turned to the back door, grabbed a staff and lantern before she offered a polite, "If you wish to speak to the dead, please follow me."

The teens scrambled up off the floor and were at her heels a moment later.

She paused near the door to the gardens. "The doors here are warded. No spectres can pass through without the help of a Death Keeper."

She turned and addressed them, giving them the basics of what it meant to be a Death Keeper.

A young woman put up her hand. "Isn't it all the same guild?"

Imara smiled. "No. Death Keepers answer to their own guild before the Mage Guild is allowed near them. It is a specialized position, and the Death Keepers can override a Mage Guild decision. There aren't enough folk with a talent for death."

A young woman with blue and green stripes in her hair asked, "Why do we even need Death Keepers?"

"We will figure that out tonight. Now, follow me and we will wake the spectres."

She fired up the staff and walked through the wards, waiting for her group to step through the glowing glyphs and join her on the other side.

Imara stifled laughter as some rushed, some jumped, and a few closed their eyes and took one giant step. When Benny, Freddy, and Sandy were all on the correct side, Imara continued her lecture.

"When a mage has prepared for their spectre to be generated, they are sent to the crystal at the moment of death. In that moment, their magic transfers instead of simply disappearing into the ether. A copy of what they know, how they know it, and all of their personal memories are placed in the crystal. That crystal is then taken and secured to an obelisk, statue, or headstone of the deceased's choosing."

She led them to the recent portion of the memorial garden. "The spectres here are awake, conscious, and able to speak to me normally, and you, if I boost their situation a little."

"Why can you speak to them all the time?"

"I am a Death Keeper. Speaking to the

dead is what comes naturally." She walked slowly to the nearest monuments, and she activated the spectres to full energy.

The girls gasped as the spectres approached, but when they paused and looked at Imara, she inclined her head. "Thank you. These young ladies are mage guides, and I would like you to speak politely with them or not at all."

The spectres nodded.

The mage guides looked confused.

"You are welcome to ask them anything. They know how they lived and how they died and are not shy about anything in between."

With that stated, the bravest of the girls went first, and she spoke to one of the spectres who was a mage that specialized in investment banking.

Benny came up next to her. "There aren't a lot of high guild spectres."

"No. They are kept at a separate facility until they fade. They are dangerous until they get to the fading point. Then, and only then, are they retired to one of these places to slowly bleed off."

Benny chuckled. "I should take notes."

"Why?"

"Because my XIA team and I are coming back tomorrow night for the same tour."

Imara laughed, but Benny was serious.

After fifteen minutes, she faded the spectres back to their normal states.

The girls drifted toward her, and they were all remarkably enthusiastic.

"Now, for a demonstration of what a Death Keeper can actually achieve, we are going to meet a Mage who passed on over one hundred and forty years ago."

She led them past the aging stones and to the section where the instructional mage waited. Imara powered her to full physicality and smiled as the woman touched the stone her crystal was embedded in.

The guides gasped in shock, and the woman gave Imara a wry look. "Thank you, Death Keeper. You have made my last night honourable."

"Thank you, Mage. You are giving these guides a night to remember. Ladies, ask her what you will. Mage Echoheart used to be an instructor, so she can offer you help in a variety of subjects."

The mage blushed.

The Guides rushed forward to ask questions, and Imara hung back.

Freddy pushed up next to her and whispered, "I have seen Death Keepers work before, but I have never seen them make a solid spectre."

"You have seen it now. We all have different talents. This just happens to be mine." Imara stood with her lantern lit, and the darkness pushed back from the gathering.

She had her own question to ask. "Freddy, you are a hellhound?"

Freddy jolted. "I know Benny didn't tell you."

"No. Not by name, but now, I know she was referring to you when she mentioned a friend who was an obligated familiar."

"Yeah, that is me. I found out when I was young. Any moment I can be hauled across the world where my mage is. Lately, she has been using me in familiar battles with other mages. It sucks."

"She makes you fight?"

"She bets on me. I have always had a strong draw to the demon zone energy, and it gives me multiple forms."

Imara reached up and stroked Mr. E's fuzzy head. "Yeah, I know something about that. If there is any way I can intercede with your mage, let me know."

Freddy looked at her in surprise. "You would do that?"

"Of course. You are a friend of a friend. I will help you any way I can but, please, understand that my skills are limited."

Mr. E snorted on her shoulder.

Imara smiled. "That said, I do have a knack for getting lucky with things." She reached into her robes and withdrew one of her business cards. "Here. They can get in touch with me around the clock."

Freddy looked at the card in surprise. "You have an answering service?"

"Yeah. I am in classes a lot, so if it is urgent, they put the call through. I am free most evenings, though, if you just wanted to get together to discuss stuff. I mean, I know you probably know more about your situation than I do, but I am willing to talk or listen."

"Thanks." Freddy looked bemused.

"How old are you, anyway?"

"Does it matter?"

"No, I suppose it doesn't. Thanks for this." Freddy opened the small purse she was carrying and tucked the card inside.

"You are welcome."

Freddy blushed. "This is going to sound weird, but can I hold onto your kitten for a while?"

Imara checked with Mr. E, and as he was fine with it, she reached up and handed her familiar over.

Freddy cuddled the kitten and whispered to him, pausing to hear his answers as he nodded and purred.

Imara watched the mage guides interacting with the spectre, and she smiled at the enthusiasm of both parties.

Benny moved close. "Why is she solid?"

"Because I gave her what she needed to become solid."

"That easy?"

"For me, but that is what I do. My body projects spectral energy, and I passively wake those that I am around. I can also focus it."

Benny blinked. "That... so that is how you did the trick with the stone?"

"Yeah, I kept draining the energy, and it was burning my skin, so I had to put energy into it, and that just led to a weird cycle. Thanks again for the ride to Ritual Space."

"No problem. It was nice to have another girl in the car." Benny grinned and then whispered, "What is Freddy doing?"

"Having a conversation with another familiar. I am afraid that I don't have clearance to listen in."

Benny nodded. "Right. Of course. How long are you going to let the kids keep getting spell techniques from the instructor?"

"She isn't giving them all the techniques. Each is missing a piece. If they try a spell, it won't come to anything. No flash, no bang, no nothing."

The guide master gave her a nod, and she stepped forward. "Ladies, please thank the Master Mage for her time."

The guides filed up to the spectre and gave her bows of respect. The spectre nodded in return and had a smile on her face.

When the guides were filing back toward the welcome centre, Imara looked to the mage. "So, do you still want to fade right now?"

The woman shook her head. "The guide master said she will bring the girls back in a few weeks for a follow-up presentation about what they learned. I want to be here for that."

Imara smiled. "Then, I will leave you a little less solid than you are now but still able to generate a hug if you want to."

"Thank you, Master Imara. Is Mirrin your family name?"

Imara touched the woman's shoulder and thinned the spectre's density slightly. "It is all the family who would claim me. Enjoy your waking hours. Talk to the other spectres. Your range extends to most of the corners of the gardens, so simply contemplate magic in all its forms."

"You are surprisingly wise for one so young."

"I have had good teachers."

The mage smiled. "That is all that I ever wished for my students. I wished that they thought of me as a good teacher."

Imara grinned. "I think that you underestimate your impact. Do you remember a mage named Reegar?"

The woman paused. "I do. He was cranky, irritable, and never followed instructions."

"His spectre remembers you fondly as the best teacher he ever had." Imara smiled.

The mage gasped and tears formed in the spectre's eyes. "Thank you."

Imara inclined her head, and she walked back to the welcome centre where the last of the group was passing through the wards. The moment that Imara passed through, she felt a pressure on the magic around her. She turned to focus on the energy, but it was gone.

The shiver that ran up her spine remained active as she turned and thanked the mage guides for coming.

Sandy made sure that they all gave proper thanks to Imara.

When the young women were gone, Freddy turned to Imara. "Here you go. Thanks for letting me talk to him. Not all mages would have."

"He sometimes needs to let off a little

steam as well. He was not truly impressed with the body he got stuck
with."

Freddy nodded. "I totally get that. I
am a hellhound, but I also take on a chi-
huahua form. It is humiliating, but it
gives my mage a leg up when she puts
me in a fight. No one expects the second
form."

"That would be an effective weapon.
Does the fighting hurt?"

Benny sighed. "Join us down the road
at the all-night café, and Freddy can fill
you in."

Freddy nodded. "Please. You look like
you could use a cup of coffee."

Imara consulted Mr. E, and he was in
the mood for a pie. "We are in. I just
have to finish up here, and I will meet
you there. It is to the left of the exit, correct?"

Benny gave her a thumbs-up. "See
you in a few minutes."

Imara looked around and found Connie skulking in one of the rear offices.

"Connie, I am leaving. Feel free to resume your videos or homework or whatever."

Connie looked around and then focused on her. Imara knew that look. This woman's name was not Connie.

"Um, great. Thanks."

Imara smiled and said, "I will just lock up when I leave. I know it can be creepy to be working alone at night."

"What? Lock up? You don't have to."

"Oh, I insist." Imara turned and walked swiftly to the door. She exited, made sure that the door was closed behind her, and then, she activated the Death Keeper warding that would only allow their kind to come and go.

Did you just lock her in there?

I did. I will make a call before we get to the café and have someone come in to check on her. I don't know where the regularly assigned keeper is, but they will be needed on duty tomorrow.

Mr. E was chuckling, but then, he was watching the door to the welcome centre.

She is trying to get through the wards with a chair.

Fascinating. That isn't going to work.

She doesn't appear to know that.

Imara got into her vehicle and opened her phone. A few minutes of chatting to the dispatch office, letting them know that there was an incursion into their territory and then she was off in search of pie and a cup of coffee. Oh, and a slice of pie for herself.

Chapter Three

The café was bright, cheerful, and filled with non-humans. Imara paused at the door, identified where Benny and Freddy were, and headed toward them.

Benny looked at Imara, looked around, and grinned. "You found us all right."

"Yes. Sorry I was late. Administrative issue."

"Have a seat." Freddy scooted over to the side so that Imara could take up the empty space.

She sat and set Mr. E down on the table. "This place is really jumping."

Benny smirked. "The side effect of a

nocturnal lifestyle. Are you all right with so many non-humans around you?"

Imara nodded. "Yes. It is just a shock after the college. You almost forget that anyone else exists."

Freddy agreed. "It was like that when I was taking journalism. Everybody was either a mage or a human. It was a relief to get over to Benny's house for a touch of the extranatural. Her family never disappointed."

Benny grinned. "I am still getting used to my dad having days where he is looking human. It is quite a change."

"What did he look like other times?"

Benny snickered as the waitress poured the coffee. "A demon. He was an incubus, and I am amazed that my parents never had more children than just little old me, but that was not in the cards."

"Is your mom human?" Imara took her cup of coffee and added cream and sugar.

"She looks human. That is enough for most folks. Her line has wolves, vampires, fey, and there is rumour of a troll."

It was apparent that Benny was proud of her heritage. There was no reason not to be.

The server came around again, so Imara ordered a slice and a whole coconut cream pie.

Freddy asked, "Are you hungry?"

"Mr. E has a sweet tooth. He also likes to chase bubbles. Jumping into the occasional pie isn't doing him any harm." Imara scratched him behind his ears.

Benny and Freddy were eating something more substantial.

It appeared that they hadn't quite gotten the idea of Mr. E and his appetite because when the pie and the slice arrived, they squealed in delight when he leaped into the centre of the pie and started eating his way out.

The laughter from the other patrons around them told Imara that Mr. E had an audience. She ate her pie, and he ate his while Benny and Freddy played with him, putting globs of whipping cream on his nose to watch him lick it off.

Mr. E didn't mind. He was going to get all that cream anyway.

Imara sipped at her coffee, and as she sat in the good humour and giggles that flowed around her, she checked her phone, and the intruder was in custody. The message from the guild was clear. The Death Keeper who was supposed to be on duty was missing.

Imara sighed and returned to her coffee.

Benny glanced at her. "Bad news?"

"The woman in the welcome centre wasn't a Death Keeper. She was a stand-in or a thief. I don't know which one. I do know that the actual keeper who was supposed to be on duty is missing."

Benny looked concerned. "Do you know them?"

Imara shook her head. "No. We don't usually socialize. The only Death Keeper I had met before I joined the college was my master in Sakenta City."

Freddy blinked. "You don't have guild meetings?"

"No. There aren't enough of us. There are barely enough to man the memorial gardens. That is why they are so far from cities, though that is where most of their population comes from. They have to increase their access while increasing their distance from population centres."

Benny blinked. "That is... weird. So, you don't have to go to class?"

"No. This is on-the-job training. If you have a talent for it, you have a talent for it. That is all."

Imara finished her coffee and looked at her kitten. He was sitting in an empty pie plate and beginning the laborious process of getting all the coconut and whipped cream off his black fuzz.

Freddy sat back. "Dang. If I had known that, I might have tried for it."

Benny smiled. "You aren't suited to it. You are firmly on the side of life at all times."

Imara glanced from one to the other, and she could almost visualize the spiritual tie between them. "You have been friends for a very long time."

Freddy wrinkled her nose. "Don't put it that way."

"Sorry. I meant that I can see the link between you."

Benny smirked. "Freddy became my friend in kindergarten. She has been defending me against those who would think harshly of me for my entire life. She is an amazing bully repellent."

Imara grinned. "I can see why. She is a force of will."

Freddy grimaced. "I have to be when I can be. I could be summoned by my mage at any moment, and that tension drives me nuts. It is not something that makes me sleep easy."

Imara nodded, and she reached out to stroke Mr. E's clean, damp fur. "I understand."

Freddy smiled. "If it makes you feel better, he doesn't care that you are bound to him. He is exceptionally impressed with your skills and your determination. He is honoured to be your familiar."

"Good. I am honoured to be his mage, so it works out well." Imara smiled.

Benny laughed, "Well, I get the pleasure of your company twice this week. Tomorrow, three XIA teams will be with us, including my own."

"Oh. Wonderful. It will be nice to see your mates again."

Freddy spluttered. "Really? You just

say it like that?"

Imara blinked. "She is not human, and she has shifters in her circle, so she has mates, not husbands. Partners, if you will."

Benny grinned, and her eyes glowed. "So, you know that too."

Imara wrinkled her nose. "Your magic isn't human magic. It isn't standard mage magic. I knew it when I first met you."

Benny nodded. "It makes sense, considering your talent. I mean, you know about some of my ancestries."

"Yes, I do. It makes sense now." She grinned.

Freddy snorted. "So, Imara, what are you doing for the rest of the night?"

"I am heading home, getting some more studying in for my final course and then getting some sleep."

Freddy blinked. "You are still in school?"

"I am finishing my qualifiers at Depford College. When I have this last course done, I will be able to get my commercial magic license."

Freddy whistled. "Wow. That is a hard rating to get."

"I know. That is why I went for it in this way. I have taken every high-credit course I could find in order to make this go as fast as I could, and there is only one left to go. Not many folks get through the course or even try it, but I am confident that I can get it done and gain some insight while I am doing it."

Benny looked up from her fries. "What is the course?"

"Spell crafting."

Freddy cackled. "She should meet Minnie."

Benny finished her food. "You know, I think you are right. What are you doing right now, Imara?"

She blinked. "Uh, wiping the last of

the whipping cream from my cat?"

"Come with us to the city, and we will introduce you to a friend of ours." Benny winked. "If we are lucky, we might meet her dragon."

"A dragon?" Imara blinked.

"Oh, I do love those mythical shifters. They get me all tingly. Benny occasionally works with a gryphon, and he sets my hellhound on fire." Freddy sighed wistfully.

Imara smiled. "You don't say."

Benny chuckled. "Imara has met him a time or two. She understands."

"I do, I really do." Imara chuckled.

Benny grinned. "Wonderful. Freddy, you be her co-pilot, and I will lead the way. If we get lost, you can tell her where we are headed."

Freddy nodded. "Will do."

The server slid their bills in front of them, and Benny grabbed them all. "I have got this."

44

Imara scowled. "I can get my own."

Benny shook her head. "It is my pleasure to get you the pie and coffee. The XIA owes you a lot more than that."

"I get paid. I get paid quite a bit. I wish folks would let me spend my money." Imara snorted as Benny handed the server the cash.

Benny grinned. "We are going to a shop next. You can spend your money there."

They were on their way when Imara asked Freddy, "Who are we going to meet?"

"Our friend Minerva. She is in town from Corudet City and working on taking inventory at an herb shop. She's a master mage and an excellent judge of character. Also, she is married to a dragon. It's a sweet story."

"It sounds like it. Do you have a romantic attachment?"

45

Freddy smiled. "Aside from drooling over the gryphon with the dreamy eyes? Nope. I can't. I have to be available to my mage."

"That sucks." She kept her vision on the red sports car that Benny was driving.

"It does. So, do you know any available mages who don't have familiars?"

Imara scratched Mr. E's ears. "No. I don't socialize much, but I could ask my mother. What are your criteria?"

"Seriously? It has to be a human mage or I would have asked Benny's family. I can't get my family to ask around. We are bound by a geas. No call for help is allowed from us to another mage unless they approach us first."

"So, because I asked, you can tell me?"

Freddy nodded. "Correct."

After a few minutes of chitchat, they pulled into the parking lot of Sawberry's

Magical Supply. The door said CLOSED, but there was light inside.

Benny got out of her car, and she beckoned for them to come to the door. Imara shrugged and got out of her car. Freddy followed, and soon, they were at the door where Benny was texting frantically.

A moment after she finished the texting, the door opened. A tall woman, who radiated power, was standing at the entrance. "Come in. I have some tea brewing."

Benny reached out and hugged the heavily pregnant woman. "Minerva. It is so good to see you again."

The energy that Minerva was exuding was far more than the average master mage. To Imara's senses, it was nearer to the power of a sun.

Freddy hugged the woman next, and then, it was Imara's turn to greet her. She inclined her head. "Pardon my lack of hug."

Minerva smiled slightly. "Thank you, and you are pardoned. I am Minerva."

"Imara."

"Death Keeper?"

"Yes. It pays for schooling."

Minerva cocked her head. "Deity in the bloodlines?"

Imara shook her head. "Not that I know of."

"Huh. Well, please come in. I am guessing that you are the reason that they came to visit."

"I am. I am taking a spell crafting course at Depford College, and they immediately thought of you."

Minerva nodded. "That would do it. Please, come in and have a seat. I am in the process of purchasing this shop, so I am doing inventory. The wards dissuade anyone who wants to nag me, and it sends them off to the next shop."

The interior of the shop was neat and

tidy for the most part, but the scent of herbs and the feel of magic were heavy in the air.

The woman walked slowly to the circle of comfy chairs, and she lowered herself into one of the seats. "Someone else pour, please."

Benny sat and took the pot into her very competent hands. "Here. When are you due?"

Minerva chuckled. "By human standards, three weeks ago. By dragon standards, I still have two months to go."

Imara asked, "So he is really a dragon?"

She sighed and inhaled the fumes from the teacup that Benny handed her. "He really is. Zemuel has his territory in Corudet City, but I have decided that my child needs more than just his empire in its life. This shop will give me a reason to come visit as well as an outlet for the child to work when it is of age."

Freddy grinned. "Nothing like looking ahead... way ahead."

Imara smiled softly. "It is good that you are planning for their life. Even if things change, it is alterations to an existing design."

Minerva looked at Imara and grinned. "I like you. So, I am going to give you the best advice I can. When you get assignments to make spells and potions, look at the ingredients and think of what they mean to *you*. The meaning in your mind will determine the end result, no matter the dictates in the spell book. If you think of sunny days when you see a sunflower, it will make the spell brighter and happier. If you look at a lily and remember a funeral, it will darken and mute the effect of the spell. You have to put all of your focus in it and realize that there is no incorrect spell, just an undesired result. By concentrating on the ingredients, you can guess at what the spell will achieve or what it won't."

That made so much sense; it explained why the strongest magical sensing strips that she had ever made were made with her favourite paper. "Thank you. That explains a lot."

"You are welcome. Is that your familiar?"

Mr. E crept out from behind Imara's collar.

"It is. While I regret the shape I chose for him, I regret nothing else."

Minerva smiled as the kitten crept closer.

"Eadric the Hellborn. I never thought to see you walking free." The deep, rumbling voice came from a corner where Imara would have sworn there was no one.

The kitten sat on Imara's arm with deep formality, and he bowed.

"Imara, this is Zemuel. Zemuel, you remember my friends Benny and Freddy."

He chuckled. "Of course. Now, be-loved, you need to return to our home to rest. This flitting around in portals isn't good for you."

In a moment, Imara felt the tremen-dous power of the dragon's mind weigh-ing down on Mr. E. He met the pressure and returned it calmly and directly. Their conversation was short, but it was obvious that they were friends of a sort.

Minerva snorted. "I can rest for a day after I have the baby."

He stepped forward, and Imara was struck by the size of him. Minerva was a tall woman, but Zemuel was a huge man. He was easily over seven feet tall, and the air of power that he wore was casual as if it didn't matter to him.

"Eadric, what are you doing wearing that ridiculous form?"

Mr. E answered him on his personal frequency, and the dragon shifted his gaze to Imara. "You are one of those from the demon-mage families?"

She cocked her head. "Genetically, yes. The Deepford-Smythe line is mine. I have not looked into the ancestors that were killed."

That seemed to surprise him. "Why not?"

"I am not close to either side of my family, so I don't concern myself with the past. I can't do anything about it."

Mr. E perched on her forearm and looked smug.

Zemuel raised his brows and actually looked closely at her. "You have the air of death about you."

She quirked her lips. "I live at a college. Some of those folks don't bathe. Sorry."

Minerva barked a laugh. "I like her."

Zemuel sighed, and the communication between him and Mr. E continued for a moment. The dragon snorted, and a shot of fire was exhaled. "Fine. I will leave her alone."

Minerva's eyes went wide. "That is one impressive kitten."

Mr. E stood and fluffed his fur out a little before looking at her with big eyes and a soft *murp*.

Imara smiled. "He loves compliments."

Zemuel crossed his arms over his chest. "He always did."

Mr. E hissed.

Imara yawned. "Apologies."

Benny grinned at her. "Long day?"

"Yeah. Prepping for classes takes a lot out of me."

Freddy gave her a commiserating look. "Maybe you should head home."

Minerva hissed. "Not until she has had something to keep her alert for the drive. Give me a minute."

Minerva got to her feet with alarming speed and made her way across the shop. Zemuel was behind her, ready to catch her if his posture was any indication.

Minerva grabbed the wheeled ladder and slid it over to wherever she was targeting, and then, she began climbing. Minerva was muttering as she found a drawer and began to paw through it until she found what she was looking for. "Aha!"

She turned her head to Zemuel and murmured, "Coming down."

He held out his arms and caught her when she jumped off the ladder. He didn't stagger, but his knees bent slightly.

When he carried her back to them, she held her hand out toward Imara. "Here you go. It is a clarity stone. It will keep you alert. It is warded against detection, but I wouldn't recommend that you take it to class."

Imara smiled and took the tiny glass

pebble. "Thank you, but I wouldn't take it to class. Mr. E would eat it if I tried to cheat. He doesn't need more clarity."

He crept up to her shoulder and purred happily against her neck.

She slipped the stone into her robe pocket and inclined her head. "It has been pleasant to meet all of you, but I had best get back to the college. I have to get my supply list together for the course."

Freddy smiled. "I thought you would have it already."

"I would have, but they won't give it to us until the day before the class."

She bowed low and paused when Zemuel shifted Minerva in his arms, and he held out a card. "Here. Call us if you need us."

She reached out and took it. The card was heavy with magic. "Um, thank you."

Minerva grinned. "Let me know if you need any supplies. I can get them for you fresh and inexpensive."

Imara smiled. "Thanks again. Good evening and take it easy. That baby needs a bit of rest."

The room erupted in hugs and laughter, so Imara took that moment to escape and head for her vehicle.

Time to get home and check her email for the shopping list she needed for her course. She would apply what Minerva had told her in the class and see what following her associates could generate.

Chapter Four

She carefully put the stone in her storage cupboard in the lab and went through the list that she had gotten in her email.

You sure that you don't want to take that with you? Mr. E idly batted around the cap from an empty herb bottle.

"I am sure. This is just a quick trip, a light lecture, and then, we are on our way home again. Sorry, buddy. No pie tonight."

He sighed but hopped onto her shoulder. *Too bad. It was tasty.*

"And it was squishing through your paws for an hour. Gross."

He chuckled in her mind as she

grabbed her robes from the hook near the door.

She waved goodbye to Reegar and Bara and headed out the door. Time to talk to the dead... again.

The Death Keeper at the welcome centre was attentive, helpful, and had the necessary magic to do the job. He was deferential to her and got out of her way when she led the three XIA teams into the gardens.

This evening was different from the previous night. She was there to wake a dead suspect in a murder and get a confession from him.

She walked up to the stone, and she tapped the obelisk politely. "Excuse me, Mage Neffling. I have some folk here who would like to speak with you."

She was holding back her energy to stop other spectres from rising. She offered a bit to his spectre, and he took it.

One moment there was a vague glow on his obelisk, and the next, he was standing in full regalia with a sneer on his features. He wasn't handsome, but he wasn't ugly.

Imara nodded to Benny, "I am not part of this investigation, so I will stay off to one side. He can't make contact with you; he will be fine as long as you need to talk to him."

She faded to one side and let the agents of the XIA gather and speak with a killer who had been dead for the better part of a century.

While keeping her energy in, she opened her senses, focusing on the shadowy, fading garden. There were still nine spectres moving, but they were excited by something. She pulled her senses back in, but just as she was nearly closed off, something cruised just out of her sensory area.

She asked Mr. E, *Did you feel that?*

Yes, and it wasn't good. That was ancient and evil.

Where did it come from? She went to open her senses again.

Don't. Don't open yourself to it. You are strong but nowhere near strong enough to take that on.

I hate to say this, but I agree with you.

The XIA members were engrossed in the stories being told by the spectre, and they hadn't noticed whatever it was that had cruised by the edge of the memorial garden. The thing was gone now, so she would just hold the information until it was appropriate.

The questioning took over two hours, but finally, the questions had been answered, and the XIA was satisfied.

Benny turned to her, and she smiled. "So, another pie?"

"No. I was wrong on my timeline. My first class is two days away, but I want to spend time doing more research. It is my last class, and I don't want to blow it."

Benny nodded. "Fair enough. Thanks for this, by the way."

"Not a problem. The money is already in my account."

When she had escorted them to the front door of the welcome centre, she turned to Argus. "Did you learn what you needed to know?"

"Yes, and I got to see you in action. My heart is yours. You are a wonder to behold."

She blushed and quickly kissed him on the lips. "Go and have pie with your team. I have to get back home and think about how fast I can blow through this course."

"Good luck and well done. He told us everything."

"I am glad. It also proves that spectres can still be useful after their bodies are gone."

He hugged her and walked her to her car. Once she was tucked in, he closed her door and walked to his SUV with the other team members laughing and elbowing each other.

Benny's team was on the way to pie when Imara pulled onto the highway. They were on their way to the café, but Imara had to head home.

She was heading toward her turnoff when she saw a flash of midnight green.

The car crunched as it was struck and flipped into a rapid roll that had Imara holding her breath and trying to gain access to her location.

She wanted to scream, but her thoughts were shorted by the sudden thud of her head into the window glass.

She heard a hiss next to her, but a roar from Mr. E's hellcat form seemed to freak out the attacker. There was a rumble of growling and hissing, but when Imara touched her head, she felt the ribbon of blood that was wrecking her robes.

She was lying upside down with light blazing into the side of her car, but she didn't know what was casting that light.

"Imara! Imara, stay still." Argus was concerned. How sweet.

She didn't turn her head to look, but she croaked, "I am seat belted in. I am not going anywhere right now. Where is Mr. E? Can someone find my cat? Please." Tears started to run up and over her forehead.

One of Argus's team said he would follow the crash through the woods.

There was a low growl, and a cranky Argus pulled the door to her driver's side away. He reached in, and his claws severed the seatbelt, catching her in his arms. He eased her out of the car, and he asked her over and over if her arms or legs could move. Once she wiggled everything to his satisfaction, he gave her a tight hug.

She looked up at him and caressed his cheek. "Something hit me."

"We know. We can see it; we can smell it. It was big and serpentine."

"Well. Shit."

The vampire brought Mr. E back. His hair was matted in places, but he was in one piece.

Imara, I am so sorry that you were targeted.

So, I was a target. That is what it felt like.

I wish I could say it was the last time.

I got lucky in that I was able to wound it, but it will be back. Her kind is always fixated.

What is she?

Argus lifted his head, and he sniffed. "Lamia."

"What?"

"She is part woman, part snake, and known for being particularly hostile when she believes she has been wronged."

"I guess I pissed someone off."

"I guess. I am taking you to the hospital."

She leaned against his shoulder and cuddled her kitten. "Sounds like a fabulous idea."

He got to his feet and carried her and Mr. E to the rear seat of the SUV. His team surrounded them, and soon, they were on their way to the hospital in Redbird City.

It was amazing how fast you were seen when three heavily muscled and body-armoured men carried you into the emergency room.

She was scanned, probed, and a healer came up to her, wrapping her abused

skull in gauze soaked in herbs and magic.

Mr. E was curled in her elbow, and
Argus held her other hand.

"You were exceptionally lucky; your
car is totalled, but you only have the
small cut on your forehead." Argus
smiled. "I have filed the report with your
insurance agency."

Imara lifted a hand to her head. Mr. E
was already healing her. "Huh. Did they
catch whatever hit my car?"

"No, but we have some serpentine
samples at the lab."

She sighed and swung her legs to one
side. "I don't suppose I could get a ride
home?"

"They want to keep you for another
day."

She glared at him. "I want to be
home."

He squeezed her hand. "I will check
with the doctor. If he says you can go, I

will take you home."

She smiled and nodded. "Thanks. I will stay here."

"So will I." He lifted his hand and jerked his head.

Imara carefully turned in time to see Lio leaving the doorway. Ivar was still standing guard.

"They are still here?"

"They are hoping that when you graduate, you are willing to join our team."

She wrinkled her nose. "I am not going to join the team the way that Benny has."

He winked. "Good. I am not up for sharing you. We want you for your magic."

Imara nodded carefully. "I know. I promise to make you a priority, but I am not going to cruise around with you every night. There are folk who want to talk to the dead, and they are willing to pay for it."

"Do you have to do that at night?"

She grinned. "Thanks for asking. No, it doesn't have to be at night, but it is easier to see the spectres after dark. They glow."

He grinned. "I don't know why I never asked that question before."

"Most folks just think that spectres are like ghosts. That they need the person seeing them to let down their mental defenses, usually via fatigue."

"Have you met a ghost?"

She grimaced. "Several. They are generally unpleasant and unhappy with their situation."

She tried to get out of the exam bed, but he tightened his grip on her hand.

"Stay where you are until the doctor releases you."

He's right you know. You could have been killed and then where would I be? Getting the stink-eye from a kitten made

69

it all the more profound.

She scratched Mr. E behind the ears. "I am not trying to hasten your next job. Sorry for the close call, and Argus, thanks for pulling me out of the wreck."

He lifted her hand to his lips. "You gave me a heart attack when your car flipped like that."

"My heart had some unusual activity in that moment as well." She felt her fingers shaking in his grip. "How messed up was my car?"

Ivar muttered from the doorway, "I am amazed you are upright. The roof was crushed into the back of the driver's seat."

She shivered again, but this time, Argus held her hand in both of his, and he pressed his forehead to the back of her wrist.

"You are fine. You survived, and you will continue to be well, or I will station a watch outside Reegar Hall."

She chuckled and bent her head to his, pressing the un-lacerated part of her forehead against his hair. They remained like that until Lio returned with the doctor.

She blinked slowly as she straightened and got a good look at him. The third eye that he sported told her one thing that she hadn't noticed earlier. She was at an extranatural hospital.

"Well, you have had a nasty knock on the head; we were going to give you stitches, but the wound started sealing itself. Your familiar is very powerful and adorable." The doctor smiled. He removed her bandage and nodded. "You have some bruising, but it is healing."

She sighed. "Good. So, I can go home?"

"I would prefer that you remain under observation tonight."

She gave him a serious look. "I would rather be home. I can arrange to have someone wake me up on the hour if necessary."

He frowned and glanced at Argus. "Will you be there?"

Argus shook his head. "No, but she does have housemates who would do that for her."

The doctor nodded. "I want you to go to a medical centre tomorrow and get a full workup. I will give you the tests I need run to close your file."

"What happens if I don't get the tests run?"

"I notify the XIA, they notify the Mage Guild, and they will put a mark in your file regarding lack of concern for your own safety."

Imara gave him a dark look. "They talked about me while I was in for scans."

The doctor looked smug. "They are chatty as hell when they are worried."

"Fine. Medical check tomorrow to

confirm that I am healed."

"Excellent. In that case, I will fill out the discharge form, and you can be on your way."

She nodded and smiled until he left, and then, she made a face.

Argus laughed and asked, "What was that expression about?"

She cuddled Mr. E. "Never ask a woman to be excited about discharge."

It was Ivar that caught the reference first, and he snorted and then hooted with laughter. Lio caught on next, and Argus just gave her a look that said she should be embarrassed by the pun.

Imara didn't care what they thought. She got to go home that night, and a few hours earlier that had not been a sure thing.

Chapter Five

*T*he XIA had driven her to Ritual Space where Hyl and Adrea had sent her home. Reegar had popped in like clockwork every hour until noon, and her medical scans were completed and sent to the hospital she had attended the night before. Since her tasks were complete, it was time to meet Kitty for a late lunch.

It took longer to walk to the café than it would have to drive to it, but when she met with Kitty, she didn't mention the accident. Kitty's news was extremely exciting.

"They want my bees!" She leaned forward and whispered it while the server was busy with their coffee.

"Really? Who?"

Kitty smiled. "The Mage Guild. They looked at the trials of our honey, and now, they want the bees."

"Our honey?"

"Mine and the bees." She grinned.

"Interesting. What are they going to do with them?"

Kitty shrugged. "I don't know. I expect they will be transported somewhere to live out their lives making magical honey."

"I hope that you are right. At least you got an excellent mark."

"I truly did. We used a split up at the farm to start our own hive. They are thriving."

Imara smiled as the server returned with their coffee. "Thank goodness. You worked hard with them; you deserve to have a portion of your efforts as a reward."

Kitty smiled and then she paused. "Are you all right? You seem a little dull today."

"Wow. That is direct."

"Did something happen?"

Imara wrinkled her nose. "Yes, I wrecked my car. Totalled it. Flipped it right over. I am fine, but it was a bit of a shock."

"When?"

"Last night."

Kitty's eyes went wide, but she kept her questions to herself until the burgers showed up.

Once they were eating, she interspersed her questions with her own consumption, and when she had assured herself that Imara was fine, she seemed to come to some kind of a decision.

"Take my car if you need it."

"You mean the truck?"

"Yeah. If you need it for a job, let me know."

76

Imara smiled. "Thank you. I think I am going to take a leave from my Death Keeper duties. I want to finish this last course strong."

"Smart."

Imara acted as she thought about it. "In fact... there, I have sent the text to the guild hall. They will spread the news."

She set her cell phone aside and gave Kitty her full attention. "How is the family?"

"I can't believe the change in grandma. She blushes, she flirts with grandpa's spectre, and they disappear for hours on end. It is so sweet."

Imara laughed. "They were definitely very much in love. How are your orbs?"

"My father and mother are letting me take the count down to five."

"That is progress."

"Yes. They still want me to be able to know what is coming but are not as wor-

77

ried about my ability to deal with shocks and surprises."

Imara smiled. "I think you have proven that you can handle yourself."

"I try, but I always seem to fall short. Master Reegar offered me a place at Reegar Hall when you have left." The last came out in a rush.

The laughter was genuine. "Your family agreed?"

"They did. Since he has you as a reference, there was no need for them to worry."

"They mentioned that they talked to me?"

"Of course."

Imara sighed. She had hoped to keep her interference behind the scenes, but now that it was out, she was glad that Reegar and Bara would have someone else to call family.

"Are you looking forward to it?"

"I am. I think we are all going to miss

you, so it will be nice to have all of us together."

The expression on Kitigan's face was happy but sweetly sad at the same time.

"Don't get ahead of yourself. I haven't left yet. One term to go."

Kitty grinned. "I am glad of it. Hopefully, we can get together a few more times. Will you be graduating?"

"I am going to be finishing out of season. I would rather just throw a small party and have friends, Luken, and my mom in attendance."

"That sounds nice. Any particular venue?"

"It would have to be Reegar Hall if Reegar wanted to be there, or Ritual Space if he didn't. That is if I pass my class. I am going to try my best, but it does take weird turns once you start aiming for a position in the Mage Guild."

Kitty nodded soberly. "I wish you nothing but the best."

"I hope your wish isn't needed."

Kitty raised her coffee in a salute. "So do I."

Imara called Argus and left a message, telling him that she was fine and she was starting classes the next day. He could call her or text her in the evening. She headed to bed and went over her applications to the guild and for her magic license.

Mr. E murmured, *Where do you think he is?*

"He is either doing paperwork or thinking about it. I think he's mad about my accident."

He is not mad. He was worried. I was furious. That creature was trying to kill you.

"I can't be sure of that."

I can. It said so.

She linked with his memory and saw the altercation. Nearly twenty feet of coils, some pale limbs but the face was in shadow. Imara heard the hiss, "She will die, and you will be vulnerable."

Imara blinked as her vision returned to the room around her. "Huh. So, it wants to kill me, but you are what it is after. Why?"

I killed a lot of people. Perhaps this is a relative.

"Really? You killed a lamia's family?"

He paused. *I thought it was a naga.*

"Not enough heads."

There was a demon who had a lamia as a lover. I killed him. She got away.

"That lacked foresight."

Yes, it did. I am sorry she came after you.

Imara rubbed her forehead where the cut had been. "So am I. I am in no mood to play with a nearly immortal shifter."

Are you all right?

"My head still hurts. I don't recover from a cracked skull like I should."

He pushed himself up against her arm, and he sent her extra energy. The burst helped the ache, but it didn't dissipate it completely.

"Thank you."

It didn't help, did it?

"It helped a bit."

He leaned against her and shared the warmth of his little body. The gentle touch helped her more than the shared energy.

She set her paperwork aside and flicked off the light. "Just one more course."

Maybe you should see the doctors again.

"I will think about it after class. For now, I just want to get some sleep and get to class tomorrow morning."

I will be with you. I always loved spell work.

She chuckled. "I know."

As Imara fell asleep, she watched Mr.

E's memories of spell work like a movie, and the power and enthusiasm that she felt gave her hope for the following day.

"I am Master Mage Midian. I will be learning what you know about crafting a spell and using the ingredients on your list. This is a master-level class, and if you feel that your skills are not up to it, I would suggest you leave now."

Imara looked around and only saw three other students.

"I also do not encourage the use of familiars, as when you need to craft a spell, you might not have access to your companion. Please, place all of the creatures in the holding area behind the curtain. I am not cruel enough to keep them from you entirely." Midian nodded.

Imara went and carried Mr. E to a nice basket behind a curtain. "Here you go, dude. Enjoy your nap."

I wish that I could have played.

"I know." She scratched his chin and headed back to the class. Two of the other students also stowed their familiars. One had an owl, the other had a ferret.

She returned to her workstation and kept her hands at her sides.

"We are a small group, so I would ask you to introduce yourselves." Master Midian paused by Imara's station. "You first."

"I am Imara Mirrin, Master Death Keeper."

"Really?"

"Yes, Master Midian. I gained Master status several months ago."

"What do you do for fun?"

Imara cocked her head. "I go out with friends; I do some consulting work."

"Consulting? For whom?" The master kept her face pleasant.

"The Mage Guild and the XIA. Occasionally, I take tours of mage guides around memorial gardens to introduce them to the possibility of working with the dead."

Master Midian nodded with an impressed grimace and moved to the next student.

Carlos Roderick was a ninth generation mage, and he wanted to take the spell crafting course in order to gain a skill that none of his family could master.

Libirak Nolthin wanted to learn how to make spells that could benefit the world.

Margo Pograth was a mage guide leader, and she wanted to set a good example for those who looked to her as a role model.

Imara suddenly wished she could change her answer.

"Excellent. Now, in front of you is a box, and inside of that box is a series of ingredients. I want you to use all of them, and anything you wish that you brought from your list."

The master walked back to her desk. "You have two hours, and you can use any of the tomes in the room, as well as all the equipment. You can begin now."

Imara stepped forward and opened the box. Her lips quirked when she took in the sight of the contents. She bent and got her notebook out, clicked her pencil, and got to work.

Class was now in session.

Chapter Six

Imara slowly stirred the beaker with a glass rod. All of the ingredients from the box had been noted and were now suspended in the liquid.

The scramble to get started had been stilted. The stops and starts of the other students were distracting, but it was their darting looks as they tried to guess what the other ones were up to that made Imara angry.

She inhaled the floral scents from her box, and she relaxed. It was time to add an ingredient from her own collection.

She stared at her supplies for ten minutes before she closed her eyes and reached out. When she saw what she had selected, she knew what her spell was for.

Imara jotted down the final ingredient and measured out ten flakes before dropping them into the beaker.

The liquid inside the beaker turned a soft and gentle green, so she put a strainer and a new bottle down and slowly poured the mixture into it.

When she was done, she broke down her station and washed up. She glanced at Master Midian, and it triggered the short brunette into jumping to her feet.

"Well, Master Mirrin, what have you made for me?"

Imara looked at the other students who were still deep in their preparation process. "I have created a potion with an interesting effect."

The master brought out a small silver cup. "What is the result?"

"Well, the box contained different flowers, which all had something to do with love. Some were obsessive love, some were love of self, and others were love from afar, and others were lost love. The potion is designed to lessen the effects of love and to ease the pain."

Midian nodded and took the vial from Imara's desk, pouring a measure into the silver cup. A bright streak of energy came out of the cup, and Midian grinned. "What was your ingredient from the list?"

Imara bit her lip for a moment. "Oatmeal flakes."

Midian cackled. "Gentle fibre for moving emotions through. Why did you make it into a potion?"

"The flower petals were all fresh and soft. Smashing them would have just been a work of violence they didn't deserve."

Midian looked thoughtful. "Well, your spell does what you say it does, so you are dismissed. I will see you this afternoon for the second class."

Imara blinked. "That's it?"

"That's it. This afternoon we will discuss your final exam. You are going to have eight weeks to prepare it, but you will have to make the same spell with the same result three times."

Imara grabbed her bags, collected Mr. E, and walked out of the class while the others were trying to speed their efforts. "That was definitely odd."

Mr. E rode proudly on her shoulder. *I knew you had a knack for this. I could feel that you have an awareness of the ingredients. It is an intensely important part of the art of crafting magic.*

"Thanks. It just felt like the thing to do. Minerva was right. You need to let the ingredients tell you what they want and let your experience with them guide the magic."

Lucky that you met her then.

Imara smiled. "I would say so."

She was carrying on this conversation while she crossed the quad. A few of the newer students gave her strange looks, but they probably couldn't see Mr. E on her shoulder.

"I think I have to buy a new car."

That is sudden.

"Not really. Not since I saw the wreck of the car from your angle."

Ah. Maybe one of the big ones like Argus drives?

"No. That is way too expensive. I need something new so that it will at least have airbags that go off. You can help me shop online, and we will see if someone can take us around on the weekend for test drives."

You need a driver to find a car?

"Yes, it is one of the great ironies of the universe." She chuckled.

Very strange.

"Yeah, but in the modern era, I can look up something online before I go see it. It cuts down on all the running around."

Are you looking because Kitty offered you her truck?

"No, I am looking because I realized that I can't even drive across the college for a quick bite for lunch."

Ah, you feel confined.

"Hobbled. Yes."

She entered Reegar Hall and headed for the fridge.

Reegar appeared at her side and walked with her. "How was your class?"

"It was good. It was weird though. I didn't use any tomes. I just did what Minerva said to do. I listened to the ingredients."

"Minerva?"

"Yes. She is a friend of a friend. She is also in the process of purchasing one of the herbal supply shops in Redbird City."

"I knew a Minerva. Tall woman. Exceptionally smart with a weird aura."

"That does sound like her."

She put together a sandwich and made another one for Mr. E. She brought everything to the table and sat down.

Reegar poured her a glass of iced tea and brought it over. "So, tell me what you got."

She blinked. "You know the format?"

"I do. I was part of the crew that invented the course. It has been the same for the last seven decades."

She took a bite of her sandwich and swallowed. "Flowers. It was flowers."

"Oh, what kind of flowers?"

"Sunflowers, narcissus, roses, white roses, yellow roses, and gardenias." She kept eating and spoke between the pauses.

"What did you do with them? Love spell?" Reegar was grinning.

"No. We had to use one of our listed

ingredients, so I used oatmeal."

Reegar stared at her, and then, he whispered, "Genius. Letting love pass."

"Right. According to the silver cup, the spell works."

"Did you try it?"

"No, I don't have any love that I want to turn into a memory." She finished her sandwich.

"Why did you choose oatmeal?"

She sat back and sipped at her iced tea. "When I was a child, I wandered into a patch of poisoned oak. My skin burned, and the only thing that helped was oatmeal baths. I see flakes of oats, and I see comfort. There is nothing better than comfort after the love brought on by obsession or self-involvement. Also, it binds stuff and carries it away without harm."

"Wow. You know a lot about oatmeal."

She smiled. "I like it."

Mr. E finished his sandwich and curled into a ball on the plate. *Wake me when we have to go back to class.*

"Is Midian teaching your course?"

"Yes, she is."

"She's good. Fair and direct. Just what you need. There is nothing subjective in her class. Did she give you study aids?"

"No. This is a lab course. It is full days for a week and then once a week until the end of the course."

"So, why are you home?"

"Lunch break. I have to head back in half an hour."

"Ah. Well, in that case, I will keep meals ready for you."

She smiled. "Thanks. I would not have been able to get this far without your help."

Reegar put his hand on her shoulder. "Sure, you would. It just wouldn't have been as fun."

She laughed. "Fun. That is a word for it."

He chuckled. "Life in our world is odd. I know it is a jolt from Sakenta, but you are adapting well. Think of this as a transition between here and Redbird City."

"A halfway house."

"Precisely."

She looked around. "It is a very nice halfway house."

"Thank you. And thank you for letting me keep my home under control."

"Where are the other students who are supposed to be moving in?"

He waved his hand. "They will wait until you no longer need privacy and support."

She sighed. "I hate to think I am depriving someone else of this shelter."

"Don't. Kitigan is moving in next term, and she will need your advice long distance."

Imara chuckled. "She told me. I think she will be fine here, but you are going to have to make room for her bees."

He quirked his brows. "I didn't know about them."

"She doesn't know about them, but I was watching them when we did the harvesting. She is their queen. I just don't know how to tell her that. She's letting the guild take her bees and their honey."

"Huh. Then, how are they going to come here?"

Imara grinned. "They are going to follow her."

"You are sure?"

"I looked up bee behaviour, and it is definitely something that will happen. There is too much magic tying them together."

"Ah. Yeah, those things can't be broken. Well, not without one party losing their lives."

She shivered. "That isn't worth thinking about."

"No, but stupider things have happened with less reason."

Imara nodded. "Right. Life is complicated."

"More and more as you live in it." Reegar smiled. "You will get used to it. You are simply reaching the end of one goal. You need to find another."

"What?"

"You heard me. Your focus has been on attaining your license, but that is nearly within your grasp. You need to look wider. Find a new focus and gain a new purpose. Your consulting business is passive. You need a goal to reach for."

Mr. E looked up from his plate. *He is not wrong.*

"How would I even start finding something else?"

"There are counselling services offered by the college. You also might want to speak with the XIA or the Mage Guild and ask if they have any programs or if the can use your services on a more regular basis."

"Oh. Right. I forgot about that."

"Or even possibly run your own garden of rest. You are a master now. You can prime and create spectres. There are many options open to you. You are smart. Once you finish with today's class, get out a corkboard and start planning. Figure out what your options are and then start making a decision."

She nodded. "Thanks for the pep talk. It is helping."

Imara's headache faded, and she smiled. "Do you want to come back to class with me, Mr. E?"

No. I am fine here. I will see you after class. He yawned, got up, turned around, and sat back down on the plate.

She made a face and headed back to class. She had a lot to think about, and the walk would do her good.

Chapter Seven

"Well, we have lost Mr. Nolthin. It appears that the idea of improvisation was too much for him. We lose a lot of students on the first day, so I am very pleased to see that you have returned and that you have abided by my rules to keep your familiars out of the lab."

Mage Midian smiled and paced back and forth in front of her class. "Now, we are getting down to the details of the course."

Midian slammed her hand on the nearest lab station. "For the next five days, you will be in here all day, every day or for at least six hours if other courses interfere. I hope none of you are stupid enough to have additional courses this term."

Imara kept herself quiet and paid attention.

"After the next five days, you will have the following seven weeks to prepare a single spell. That spell will have to be what the books consider to be a *great* spell. The spell will have to be powerful, exotic, and here is the fun part... you must execute it equally three times. You will be allowed to keep one example of your spell, one will be executed in a protected space, and one will be kept in the archives."

Margo asked, "What ingredients can we use?"

"Anything you wish as long as you have enough for three spells. You can use any materials, any containers, any combination of the above, but it has to be an original spell. We will test the result against all known spells, and if you have come up with an original spell, you are fast-tracked to Master Mage status. If it is a derivative but mostly original spell, you will qualify for Senior Journeyman Mage status. A copied spell is an automatic fail."

Imara nodded.

"On the wall behind my desk is the largest collection of how-to guides for writing spells that we have located. Know your ingredients. Have fun."

Imara asked, "How are our days to be structured? Will we receive one box of ingredients per class?"

Mage Midian smiled slightly. "You can have as many boxes of ingredients as you can manage. Practice is key in mastering your ingredients."

Imara nodded. "Do you wish us to provide you with notes as to our ingredients, recipes, and the spells?"

"Yes. I would like a copy of everything

you hand in."

The students nodded, and Midian looked at them with an expectant air. "Well, the new boxes are on your workstations; you have two hours, ten minutes to create a spell from the contents within. If you find something poisonous, feel free to do something creative with it."

Imara looked over and found the box on her station. She opened the box and lined up the ingredients in even rows.

A quick glance at the other tables showed her that they all got different contents. No two boxes were the same.

Imara's ingredients were dry herbs and minerals. She got her notebook out and started to make notes as she started with the lapis lazuli and a mortar and pestle.

Sweat dripped into the mortar containing the multicoloured sand comprised of herbs, flowers, and rocks. The sweat activated a tiny cascade in the mortar, so Imara called it quits.

Now came the tricky part. She took a piece of obsidian from her own collection, and she centred it above the mortar. The sand gathered around it and sank deep.

Imara watched and murmured a low, wordless chant over the work, coaxing the desert storm into the obsidian.

She watched as it began to swirl and twist, pulling the ingredients down into the stone. The obsidian was shiny, and the storm of sand was visible inside the glass.

Imara lifted the stone out of the mortar, and she set it on a soft chamois. Midian was at her station before Imara could wash out her mortar.

"So, what do we have now?"

Imara smiled. "I think it is a desert storm."

"Not very useful." Midian looked at it and frowned.

"I am working through some personal issues, so this reflects my current state of mind."

"Ah. Well, let's see if it is what you think it is." The mage picked up the stone and eased it into her silver cup.

The roar of wind that spiralled out of the cup accompanied the whirl of light.

"Well, you have definitely created a solid spell here. This is a concealment spell mixed with a sandstorm. Well done. Partial marks as you didn't know about the other half of your spell, but good start, Death Keeper Mirrin."

Imara sighed. "Thank you."

"Clean up and go home. You look wiped out."

Imara nodded. "Halfway there."

She finished up, watched that the master was putting her stone in one of three boxes near the window, Imara guessed that it was what would become her collection.

Midian smiled slightly, and another box appeared on Imara's desk. With a glance at the clock, Imara opened the box and started her next spell.

She paused and smelled each of the items and smiled. That was what she was creating, a spell to ease laughter into the world. Since scent had tipped her off, she was making a concentrated oil to become a vapour.

It was going to be a rush to finish in time, but she knew what to do. All that studying of techniques was finally paying off.

She focused on laughter as she bruised the plants and set them into a decoction flask. They swirled around in a bright solution of purified water and saffron.

While the flame did its work to heat the herbs and release the oils, Imara worked to clean up after her previous spell.

She knew when it began to drip the oil through the small still, that she had created a flight spell. It was a dangerous spell as the euphoria that it created was not an amazing combination for the power of flight.

She kept her thoughts on the spell as she recorded the ingredients and her technique.

When she had a sixteenth of an ounce of oil, she poured the oil into a tiny vial, and she capped it. She took the rest of the herbs off the flame and disposed of them.

Midian had been checking on Carlos, but she changed direction when Imara was washing up.

"What do you have now?"

Imara looked at the clock. She had five minutes to spare. "Icarus oil."

Midian blinked. "What?"

"A levitation potion that elicits elevat-ed mood as well as the physical side ef-fect." She handed over the vial.

Once again, the silver cup came out, and when a drop struck the bottom, the energy in the cup sent a cascade of golds and yellows skyward with enough force to jar the cup from the mage's hand.

Master Midian stared at the cup. "You didn't make a lot."

"No, it is dangerous. I considered it unwise to make more."

Midian nodded. "Huh. So, you are concerned with the welfare of those around you?"

"Of course. I would never want to be responsible for someone getting injured, or high, for that matter."

"And yet, you made the oil."

"It was what the ingredients wanted to be today."

"Interesting. I will see you tomorrow morning. I am working on some strange combinations that I think you can do justice to."

Imara swallowed, but her stomach filled with lead. "I look forward to it."

"Don't lie. It doesn't suit you. Dismissed for the day. See all three of you tomorrow."

The ingredients, spells, and paraphernalia disappeared from every workstation.

Margo blinked. "I was nearly done."

Carlos patted her on the shoulder. "I don't think she cares."

Midian smiled brightly. "I don't care. In your careers, if you are creating spells, or executing them, there is a time limit involved. The only time in this course that you are not held to a time limit is your final exam. It is your creation, take your time. Now... get out."

Imara nodded and left with the other two.

Carlos asked, "You come from a long

line of spell crafters?"

"I have no idea. I was fostered." She smiled brightly. "But, I do have supportive friends that have helped me to study and get my head in the right place."

Margo asked, "How could you study for this?"

"You have to focus on each ingredient and how it makes you feel. What do *you* associate with it? When you know that, you know what to do with it."

Carlos stopped. "You are joking."

"I am not. Crafting a spell is more about the mage and less about the ingredients. It makes things predictable if you work it from that angle. If you are in the mood tonight, and you have a space where you live, enchant some of your favourite spices and see what happens when you add them to bread or even just flour."

Margo snorted. "I am not even going to waste my time." She stalked past them and exited through the main doors into bright daylight.

Carlos nodded. "I don't think that kind of experiment is a waste. So, I just focus on the ingredients?"

"Focus on the way they make you feel and add magic to the mix. The rest works itself out."

He nodded. "Thanks for the tip. Can I buy you a coffee?"

They had emerged from the magic lab building and were on their way to the quad. Across the way, she saw a familiar figure. "Another time, perhaps."

She stepped away from him, and she began to jog toward the familiar figure of Argus as he was moving in her direction.

When she got to him, she shocked him by throwing her arms around his neck and pulling him down to her for a kiss, in full view of the assembled and curious students.

When she pulled back, he smiled at her with a foolish grin. "What was that for?"

"I have missed you, and I am going to be a hellish bitch for a week, so you are going to need to be scarce."

He grinned and kept his arms looped around her waist. "How would I notice?"

She punched him in the bicep. "Funny man."

"I thought it was amusing. Rough course?"

"One week of full-day classes, including weekends. I am going to be completely fried." She looped an arm around his waist. "So, what brings you here?"

"I have your insurance cheque for your car and all of your possessions. You keep a really clean car." His admiration was audible.

"It wasn't new or fancy, but it was mine. Now, I have to go looking for another one." She grimaced. "Stupid-

113

whatever-it-was."

"We are still analyzing it, but it appears to be an ancient serpentine shifter."

"Wonderful. Mr. E said it could be a lamia."

"That would be unlikely. They hunt in pairs. This was solitary, so we are guessing some kind of naga."

She wrinkled her nose. "Mr. E fought it, so I am going to trust his guess. As soon as I have a spare minute, I am looking it up as thoroughly as I can."

"I know a few people who can advise you on ancient shifters, but I don't know if they would be willing to travel here to talk to you."

She sighed. "I think I know who you mean, but I am comfortable making that call. Benny should be able to tell me what I need to know."

He nodded. "She is an excellent choice, but I was thinking of her parents.

They don't travel much though."

"Ah. Well, I will ask her anyway."

They were slowly making their way toward Reegar Hall.

"What does Reegar think of this course?"

"He knows it is necessary to reaching my goals, but he has given me some good advice."

"What is that?"

"Now that I have almost achieved a goal I set myself when I was a child, it is time to go looking for new goals and activities to focus on. I am the type of person who needs to drive themselves. Without that drive, I start to lose focus on the moment."

"I see. What is driving your public display of affection?"

She smiled. "There are two factors. The first factor is that the guy in my class was giving me looks that made me a little uncomfortable. I thought it best to nip his intentions in the bud. The second was that you are part of the new plan I need to make, so I thought I would test out public affection. I rather enjoyed it."

His voice got lower. "I did as well. It is probably a good thing that it was in a public place. My beast tried to snap my controls and fly off with you."

She grinned. "I choose my battles wisely."

Chapter Eight

The next week was a blur of calls, spells, potions, enchantments, and hot and ready lunches made by Reegar. Bara was doing Imara's laundry, and she had never felt so cared for in her life.

Master Midian was working them to exhaustion to prove to them the importance of focus and control. Margo tried to make the same spell four times in a row, and it was only when Midian eradicated all of her equipment that she had lifted her head and listened to what the instructor was telling her. She was not cut out for the improvisation of spell crafting.

Carlos, on the other hand, flourished

in the class. He worked with his instincts, and his spell work got faster and stronger. The master was impressed and watched him for a few days until it appeared that the change would stick.

Imara had never been so relieved to finish going to class as she was when she finished the spell crafting tutorial. Now, it was all about planning a spell. Reegar made her breakfast and then scowled at her while she ate. "You still don't know?"

She fed Mr. E some of the smoked salmon from her plate. "I still don't know. Nothing I have come up with has felt right, so I am going to ask folks to give me something small, and I will use those objects for the spell, with some additions that I have come across."

"A friendship spell?"

"Sort of. I have written down a few ingredients, but I will have to ask people for them."

He blinked and leaned forward. "Colour me interested. What ingredients?"

Imara sighed and pulled the folded piece of paper out of her bra, unfolding and straightening it as she went.

"Right. Well, it starts with the hair of a familiar. After that, it gets weirder, the nail of a beast, an empty soul, a moment of joy, the blood of an enemy, the word of a friend, and the will of the caster."

"That is quite the list. What do you think the spell is?"

She looked at the list and the notes she had added to the margins. She would add magic detector strips, a tiny tornado, a leaf from Ritual Space and bind it all with the enchanted honey.

She tapped her finger on the page. "I think it is a spell of need."

"What kind of need?"

"You know, I have no idea." She chuckled. "It just seemed right."

"If it seemed right, get collecting on those ingredients."

"I am going to finish breakfast first. I have a meeting to get to."

He raised his brows. "I didn't know you had a vehicle."

"I don't. I am having a meeting in Ritual Space. It is more convenient for both of us."

"Ah. Well, finish your breakfast and go. You only have a few weeks left before the course is over. Can you hand it in early?"

"I can, but she warned us against it. Mage Midian stated that this was our one chance to create a new spell and that no one benefited from rushing it."

"She isn't wrong. These shelves are full of spells that were rushed and now don't function as they should."

She finished the last caper and took her dish to the sink, washing it before setting it on the drying rack.

"Thanks for breakfast, Reegar. You have been a tremendous friend through all of this."

"I am friend to very few, but I am glad you are among them."

She leaned in and gave him a hug. He stiffened in surprise. She laughed, and Mr. E jumped to her shoulder. He smelled like fish, but it wasn't the worst thing he had smelled like since becoming her familiar. His dietary habits were ridiculous.

She headed back to her room and activated the portal to Ritual Space. She had a brunch date to keep, but she would never turn down breakfast from Reegar. He made the effort, so she was going to eat it. Getting a spectre to do any kind of domestic duty was a miracle in itself.

She sent the text through, and when she got a response, she took the step from her room to the enclosed fun park of magic and nature where mages could learn and spells could be cast with the rest of the world at a safe distance. It was also the place where Imara learned to climb walls and break into buildings. *Ah, good times.*

Adrea was standing near the portal. Benny and Freddy were at her side. Blueberry, the blue-striped bunny rabbit, was at her feet.

Mr. E was wiggling with excitement. *May I go and play?*

Imara silently spoke to him, *Doesn't it lack dignity?*

It is extremely fun.

Fine. Off you go. Enjoy yourself.

Mr. E made a happy murp and ran over to Blueberry. They looked at each other for a long moment, and then, they raced side by side to the garden at the back of the main house.

Adrea smiled. "Now that they are off playing, shall we have a spot of breakfast?"

Freddy's nose twitched. "Sure, but I

think someone already had some salmon."

Imara smiled beatifically. "Mr. E. He
is mad for it. For an ancient mage, his
beast is in control a lot of the time."

Freddy snorted. "I have *so* been
there."

Benny grinned. "Nice to see you
again. I have gotten that information for
you."

"Oh, thank you. I have been working
on finding out, but the spell crafting
class took all of my time."

"Is it over?"

"Everything but the final. I still have
to collect some stuff for that."

Adrea grinned. "Do tell but over
breakfast. We just got our blunderberry
harvest, and I can't wait for you to taste
them."

There was a charming table set for
four in the back garden, and the large
blue berries sitting on the table sur-

rounded by cream, scones, and small pancakes looked lovely.

Freddy asked the question, "What the hell is a blunderberry?"

"It was supposed to be a blueberry, but the raspberries and blackberries grew into a braided vine with the blueberry, and this was the result. It is a pretty bush, but the fruit is perplexing. Tasty though."

Adrea sat and poured tea all around. "So, what did Imara ask you to look up?"

Benny pulled a chunk of paperwork out of her purse. "Lamias. One trashed her car while she was in it on the highway."

"Oh, the accident."

"Correct."

"I thought they always hunted in pairs." Adrea smiled slightly as she offered fluffy biscuits to everyone.

Freddy split her biscuit and slathered it with the clotted cream. "That changes depending on the reason for the hunt. They mate separately, so if one lost a mate, the other wouldn't go to avenge her companion's mate."

Benny blinked. "She should have just asked you. Yeah, that is what I found out. One hunting alone has a personal vendetta against you or Mr. E."

Imara scooped up some of the berries and put them on top of the cream. "That is what I figured. I just had hoped that most of his enemies were dead."

Benny sighed. "I guess they are not."

"No, I suppose not." Imara bit the dessert, and she had to scramble to suck in all the juice from the exploding berries. Blunderberries were amazing.

The other ladies were all laughing and trying to keep themselves from looking like they had gone face first into the berry bushes.

Slurping and giggles gradually gave way to conversation, and Benny asked the loaded question, "So, what are you doing now?"

"Ah, I am working on my spell crafting course. If you speak to Minerva, please tell her that her advice has been passed on, and my classmate and I are both benefiting. The master mage is a little confused by his sudden competence, but it is going well for him."

Freddy frowned. "Only one classmate is benefiting?"

"Yeah. We started with four students. One dropped out on the first day, and the second wasn't making strides by the lab week. She was encouraged to find another occupation."

Adrea winced. "That is harsh."

"Yes, well, this is a multi-credit course, for higher class levels. You have to have a high average in your previous courses, and at least one recommendation from a faculty member."

Freddy looked impressed. "Who was

the faculty member for your recommendation?"

"My stealth magic instructor. He
signed the form while laughing."

Adrea grinned. "Hyl still talks about
you being a natural assassin."

"He is an excellent teacher."

Benny cocked her head. "What is your
final exam in your spell crafting course?"

"I have to make something that hasn't
been seen before."

"Do you have an idea of what you
want?" Benny sipped her tea.

"I do. Well, I have notes."

"Can I see them?"

Freddy grinned. "Benny was
homeschooled when it came to her spell
casting knowledge, but there are very
few people I would trust to look into
your information. Two are sitting at this
table, and one is playing house with a
dragon."

Imara fished the paper out of her bra

and handed it over.

Benny snickered. "I carry everything in there. Let me just look over this."

Benny looked at the list, glanced at Imara with raised brows a few times, and she folded the page. "We can give you three of the items on the page."

Freddy blinked. "We can?"

"Sure. Adrea can provide three leaves from Ritual Space."

"Of course."

"Freddy can pull out three hairs for the hair of a familiar," Benny smirked.

Freddy blinked. "Hey! I don't give my body parts away easily."

"I know. The thrust of this spell isn't for control over anything, it is for providing for and filling a need."

Adrea cocked her head. "What need?"

Imara answered, "Whatever the caster needs most at the moment."

"Interesting. So, the caster had better be sure of their need."

"Precisely." Imara nodded. "It isn't a spell to be used in haste."

Benny nodded and handed the page back. "I haven't seen anything like it. There are wish-fulfillment spells that come close, but this one uses something else."

Imara nodded. "Exactly. The spell uses ingredients that are enchanted by their very existence. The magic has already been *paid for* so to speak."

Adrea whistled. "That is new."

"And a little vanilla for the scent of cookies." Imara smiled.

The ladies laughed until Freddy paused. "Benny, you said that she could get three ingredients from us. What else?"

"The blood of an enemy." Benny waved her hand. "One of my ancestors arrested Mr. E all those years ago, and I have demon blood in me. Lots of it. That is enough of an enemy in the eyes of her

129

familiar, and it will work for the spell."

Imara blinked tears back. "I was just going to ask Adrea if I could retrieve the empty soul if she didn't mind."

Adrea frowned, "The... oh. Is that what that is?"

"Yes. The spectres are gone now, I can remove the stone."

"By all means. Go and get it before you leave."

"Thank you. I didn't want to remove anything from the premises without permission."

Adrea looked bright. "Can I interest you in three blunderberries instead of the leaves?"

"I don't think they would make it for a month without spoiling."

"What about dehydrated ones? The plant won't stop bearing."

"Uh, sure. That will be fine."

"Or the berries and the leaves. Please, please, take the berries!" Adrea clenched her hands together as she pleaded.

She surrendered. "Yes. Yes, of course, I will take as many as you are willing to part with."

Benny snickered. "There is a sucker born every minute."

"Says you. I am going to see if Reegar wants to try planting them outside the hall."

Adrea nodded. "I would be interested in finding out if they grow outside of Ritual Space."

"As would I. Seeing how they would grow within a spectral field would be interesting."

"I think so as well. So, I give you the seeds, and you let me know if they grow."

Imara grinned. "Deal."

Benny cleared her throat. "So, do you want to learn more about the lamia?"

"Please."

"They are creatures of myth and legend. In some cases, they are all said to be one woman who was tricked into murdering her own children, and in others, she was a seductress who lured young men in to their deaths. She can project her vision to find her prey in most legends."

Benny lifted her sheaf of papers. "In the modern era, after the wave, lamia have been sighted in pairs across every continent. There are always two, always female, and they always find each other during their first transformation."

Imara frowned. "Do they have to register?"

"No. They are only recorded if they break the law, just as the rest of the extranaturals are."

Imara nodded. "Thank you. It gives me a place to start. Someone had to have seen them around Mr. E in the past."

"Hopefully. Someone would have acted as a witness against him."

Imara sighed. "I suppose I will just have to make a trip to the archive."

She caught a glimpse of dark fur streaking across the lawn with a bunny in hot pursuit. "Hey, Mr. E, road trip!"

He made an un-kitten-like right angle, and he kept running until he was on her shoulder. *When are we going, and whose car are you going to borrow?*

She quirked her lips. "Car shopping is the next thing on my list."

Freddy nodded. "What are you going to get?"

Imara reached up and scratched Mr. E under the chin. "Something with a big dashboard."

They all laughed at the blissful kitten, and he didn't mind a bit.

Chapter Nine

Imara sat with the counsellor and seer, N'sha, and stared into her brilliant amber eyes as she learned the path her life could take.

"You are exceptionally bright, Ms. Mirrin. You have the opportunity to join the guild at the highest level. While I understand your need to strike out on your own, I urge you to take a more conventional path."

Imara held Mr. E in her lap and stroked him to soothe him and herself at the same time. This was her third meeting with the counsellor, and he was unsettled every time. Frankly, so was she.

"I know that the path isn't one that is

normally considered, but it is the one I have chosen. Thank you for the contact information for the Mage Guild enforcement and the XIA. You have helped convince me of the direction I should be looking."

N'sha leaned back. "If you are sure that this is the path you choose, I respect your decision. I do still have some feelers out for more opportunities for you. May I call you if they come in?"

Imara nodded. "Please. That would be very helpful. Any information can be put to use."

"I agree. Well, it has been interesting going over your records. I look forward to seeing you again."

Imara took the hint and got to her feet with Mr. E in her arms. "Have a good day, Counsellor N'sha."

"You as well. You have a bright future. Take care of it."

Imara left and walked through the

nearly empty halls of the Brokal Building. Named after Heinrich Brokal, it was famous for not being able to keep inhabitants in its halls. No one liked to stay in his building.

When they were outside the building, she inhaled and exhaled slowly. "I wish I knew how to get that feeling out of the walls."

There is probably a mage who can work the clearance spell, but no one wants to pay for it.

"Right. I forget that magic pays."

You had better count on it. You are about to throw yourself into that realm.

"I know. It is just hard to imagine that a dream I only developed as a frantic escape is coming true."

You have earned this moment. Enjoy it.

She nodded. There was still a week to go, but she had made up her mind. She was going to finish her spell and complete her course. There was no putting it off. This was the spell she had been meant to create.

She got into her light SUV and settled in with Mr. E hopping onto the dashboard. The Brokal Building was on the other side of campus from Reegar Hall, so driving her new car had seemed like the best option.

Mr. E enjoyed the new-car smell. None of his previous mages had driven, and if they had, they certainly hadn't taken him along with them. Imara was happy that she could give him little experiences that he enjoyed. Her happiness was tied to his.

Imara woke up and knew that it was time. After hashing and rehashing what she should use, she knew what she needed. She gathered the ingredients, set up a video camera and went to work.

The notebooks that she needed were

next to her, and with precision, she started with her first ingredients across three containers.

The first thing that she added was *soil from her mother's garden.* The soil from the site of the most recent wave.

It was done, she had started. Now to continue with *words from a friend.* Reegar had written the words *You can do this* on three sheets of parchment. She folded them carefully and set them into the three bowls.

The *empty soul* was the shattered spectre crystal from the incident where she first met Benny. When she had finished draining the spectres, the crystal had cracked into three chunks. It had offered itself to her at that moment. She thought of it as the empty soul because it had never held a soul.

The *ties that bind* had been offered by Bara. It was rope that she and Luken had made for this test. Her twin had offered his help, and Bara had put him to work. The rope was cut into three pieces and placed gently in the containers.

The rest of the pieces came together quickly, and by the time the last slip of blunderberry leaf was in, the spell was nearly complete.

She took three matches and lit each group of contents on fire, muttering about blending, binding, and melting together.

Violent purple fire shot upwards with each match touching the ingredients. She focused and murmured encouragement for the fire to give way to liquid.

The blaze turned blue then green, yellow, and finally red before it disappeared and left behind a molten and metallic gold liquid.

The honey from the magic bees was added in minute amounts. The gold liquid began to swirl rapidly, and she took out the final gift from Kitigan's family.

Three orbs of seer glass were lined up, and she used the tiny funnel to fill each of them before she corked them.

The one-and-a-half inch orbs were filled with a golden storm of potential. All the love and support that Imara had gotten for this project had humbled her. Argus had even shifted and clipped one of his claws with his beak before snipping the clipping into pieces. She had her piece of a beast.

She held her breath as she transferred the corked spells to velvet-lined, padded boxes.

When the last box was closed, she nearly collapsed. Instead, she put away the ingredients and set them up carefully on the shelves.

Keeping the lab neat was what she needed to stay sane. Once everything was complete, she checked the video and popped the chip.

She looked at the chip and pressed it

to her forehead. "Right. Done."

Master Midian had agreed to accept a video as she was out of town until late in the afternoon.

Imara gathered her boxes and notebooks, carrying everything out into the common space, and she settled them quickly into the padded and lined box that Reegar had prepared for the occasion.

The moment that she settled in the chair near the library, she heard shouts.

"Surprise!"

Bara and Luken jumped out from behind the stacks, Reegar simply appeared, and Mr. E crept out from under her chair.

Imara's heart stuttered and then fired up a pounding beat. "Oh! Thank you."

Mr. E crawled up and sat on her lap, purring up a storm. She clutched him, and her pulse immediately slowed to a more normal beat.

Bara chuckled. "You look exhausted."

Reegar nodded. "It is the most trying spell she could make, so she put everything in herself into it."

Luken came up and squeezed her hand. "You did well, sister."

"Thanks, but we don't even know if it works."

Reegar snorted. "You might get partial credit if you misidentified the spell, but you still managed to create something that radiates power. That is a pass no matter the level of it."

Imara looked at him weakly. "Really?"

"Really. I supervised your procedures, and there is no way that any of your mechanics can't be replicated. There was nothing shifty about it. That is what they are looking for."

Imara nodded. "Good."

Bara grinned. "We have cake."

"What time is it?"

142

Reegar cocked his head. "It is just after four."

She sat up. "What?"

"Yes, you have been working for eight hours without a break. Why?"

"I have to bring the spells to Midian at five."

Bara grimaced. "Have some cake. You need to eat."

Mr. E looked up at her with bright gold eyes. *I made you a present.*

She blinked. "What?"

I made you something to keep your version of the spell on. It is next to Reegar.

Reegar noted where she was looking, and he picked up the box. "Ah, yes. Your familiar made this for you. I confess to being surprised at his dexterity."

Bara smiled. "I helped a little."

Reegar handed her the box, and Imara opened it with curiosity burning in her.

A bracelet made of shining steel with a clasp and a kitten engraved on the back of it was sitting on a bed of black velvet.

"Should I put it on?"

Please. I measured it by hugging your arm while you slept.

She grinned and slipped the band over her wrist. It felt comfortable, and then, she didn't even feel it. She picked him up and got to her feet, walking over to her spells and opening one of the boxes.

"Now, how do I put this on the band?"

Luken piped up, "Just touch your spell to the clasp. It will attach automatically to the nearest link. There are concealment spells on it and comfort spells."

"Thank you, brother, and most of all, thank you, Mr. E."

Her little friend squirmed. *You de-*

144

serve more from those around you.

"I have gotten tons of support from friends and family. I am enjoying it for what it is. Affection freely given."

She checked her phone. "Damn. And now I have to run from this very touching moment."

Reegar reached in and pulled out her private notebook. "No sense in letting the mages get their hands on all copies."

"Right. Well, hopefully, I will be back in an hour or so. Mr. E, you stay here. You know how she feels about familiars."

He sighed and jumped from her arms to the table. *You really like it?*

"I really do. Talk to you soon."

Reegar frowned. "Aren't you going out with Argus tonight?"

"That isn't until eight. I have time."

She lifted the box from the table, inhaled, and said, "Wish me luck!"

Luken grinned. "I did. That is why

you were born first."

She snorted and walked out of Reegar Hall, heading for the mage labs.

Midian took the experimental spell and carried it to the testing lab. The lab was designed to mimic a human body and determine the nature of the magic itself.

"Well, Mirrin, this looks good. The spell log is solid, so now, we just have to see what it does or what the potential is."

Imara nodded, and she stood with her fingers woven together tightly. The sacrificial spell was placed on the table, and Midian left the room, placing her hand on the activation glyph and then chanting softly.

The spell shivered, shimmered and then exploded in the room, shattering and rocketing around the space until it gradually faded.

Imara didn't see any change at first. When she looked in, she suddenly noticed that everything was better. The wood was darker, the chair was pristine, the blotter had no stains and was made of a fine-grade leather where it had been rough cardboard before.

Midian smiled slowly. "Excellently done. You will be receiving an invitation to the Mage Guild by the end of the week."

To Imara's shock, Midian extended her hand. Out of reflex, she shook hands with her instructor.

The slight scratch on her finger came when she withdrew her hand. She looked at the pinprick of blood on her finger and then Midian's hand.

The snake ring seemed like something Imara should have seen before.

She stepped back and headed for the door. Midian didn't call out after her.

The main hall was bloated and flexed.

The doorway was warped, and it was nearly impossible to figure out the latch to let herself into the fresh air.

The hiss behind her made her turn. To her shock, it was N'sha's torso riding on top of the serpentine lower body. N'sha reared up to tower over her, grinning and exposing fangs dripping with venom.

The shouts coming from the quad told Imara that she wasn't imagining the horror that was slashing at her with claws as deadly as the fangs.

The burn of the claw strike on her right arm sent a shockwave through her limb and left it limp. Imara fell to the ground as the toxin spread. She tried to connect with Mr. E, but there was nothing but fury and frustration on that end.

"Oh, you can't call your little familiar. He is busy with my sister."

Panic and pain turned to worry. "Don't hurt him."

148

N'sha moved in and leaned over her, her tail snaking around Imara's body and holding her in place. "We can't hurt him, but we can hurt you, and we will."

Paralysis was moving in on her, but there was one thing that she could do. When no one human could help her, she called the spectres. They might not assist her, but it was the only move she had. She gave it everything she could.

Chapter Ten

Mage Reegar watched from the edge of his territory as the lamia hauled Mr. E away before he could run to the side of his mage. Fury and frustration ripped through him as he pounded against the barrier that bound him to Reegar Hall.

Bara and Luken came up behind him, and Bara asked, "What is wrong?"

"The lamia, they have Imara and Mr. E. They are at the mage lab."

Luken was dialling, and he gave a clipped account into the phone, and then, he did it again. "Bara, stay here."

Bara looked at him. "Like hell."

Reegar looked at them both. "Go!"

They ran.

A minute after they ran, he felt a fantastic surge of spectral energy. Reegar took one step after another, and to his determined astonishment, he was running across the lawn and heading for the broadcast point of the energy. Imara had to be there, there was no one else who could do what she did with spectres.

* * * *

Imara lay in the serpent's coils as she was inflicted with dozens of cuts. Her head remained clear, which was a deviant construct in itself.

N'sha was hissing with delight that Imara had created the spells to bind her familiar when she had made one of the privacy spells. The moment Midian saw it, she knew that it was the spell they had been looking for to bind their enemy.

Imara blinked. She knew the spell. She had made it out of cotton plants, Jell-O powder, the smoke from dry ice, and a dollop of whipped cream. It was a spell of soft silence to give her a moment of privacy from Mr. E when she was on a date with Argus. She had never considered it binding, but the power was in the heart of the mage.

A whisper came to her. "What can I do?"

She blinked. It was Reegar's voice, but he wasn't physical.

She whispered. "I have to set him free. I need to cast the last spell."

"I understand. Prepare to focus."

"It is my world right now."

She could feel the frustration and restriction that Mr. E was wrapped in, and this would make it better.

She watched her right arm lift.

N'sha blinked. "What are you doing?"

"Giving him what he needs."

Her arm was dropped across her chest, the glass shattered and the liquid seeped out. She focused and smiled. "Give him what he needs."

The lamia reared back, but Imara was beyond that. The golden energy lifted her, and it shot off to one side and struck Mr. E in the other lamia's hands.

Imara thought, *Heal his past, mend his soul, brighten his future, give him what he needs.*

The kitten was enveloped in power, and the smothering of their connection disappeared in a blaze of energy.

Imara must have passed out because when she woke up, chaos surrounded her. Argus's gryphon was wrestling with N'sha while Chancellor Deepford-Smythe was pelting the ancient creature with bursts of lightning.

Imara tried to push herself to a kneeling position, but she slipped in her own blood.

A thunderclap of magic struck on the far side of the green space, and Imara watched a strange mage levitate Midian before smashing her to the ground.

Imara gave a silent cheer and watched everything from her hands and knees.

The battles around her weren't hers. She had one fight right now, and that was to stay conscious.

"Imara... oh god. Stay still. I have something that might stop the bleeding." Bara appeared at her side, and she started wrapping the wounds.

Imara felt the burn of the slices all over her body as the wrapper tightened against her skin. She exhaled sharply but kept her silent screams to herself. Bara was helping, and she didn't need guilt.

Luken was standing next to her, and Imara could feel the protective shield that he had around her. She teared up. When another set of men came to stand with Luken, she fought a sob. Michael and Alexander Demiel joined their youngest brother, and the wall around her solidified.

Alexander turned from the defenses, and he knelt at her side. "Ah, sister. What did they do to you?"

Imara looked up at him through her exhaustion. "Whatever it was, I didn't like it."

He smiled slightly. "I got my guild status in healing. Can I help you?"

She nodded. "Sure."

"This is going to hurt."

"I expect nothing less."

Alexander chanted, focused and then wrapped her in enough energy to sear her soul. She was lifted off her hands and knees, and the burn along her nerves kept her focused until he set her on her feet.

Imara looked around and said, "Help me over to Midian. I think I can end this."

Bara took her arm. "Which one is Midian?"

Imara pointed to the one on the ground with the other mage. "Her."

They started to move as a unit toward the mage and the slowly writhing lamia.

"Can someone get me a pebble?"

Alexander bent and picked up a handful from a flowerbed that they passed on their way. "Choose one."

Imara looked at the options and grabbed two. Each was round and nearly spherical. She wasn't sure if she was strong enough to do what she was about to attempt twice, but she knew she could do it once.

"How close do we need to get?"

"I need to be within ten feet of her," Imara grunted.

Bara whispered, "Why?"

"She has something I need." Imara kept putting one foot in front of the other, and Alexander took her other arm to help support her. The contact was agony. His healing may have temporarily sealed the wounds, but the venom was still in her bloodstream. It was acid, and it would burn its way out of her. It was just a matter of time.

She felt what she needed the moment she was within range. "Stop here. I can do the rest."

Luken said, "We are not leaving you."

She gave her brother a long look. "Fine. But when we are done here, get me to the other one. She will probably come to us, but just in case, I will need to get to her as well."

He nodded.

She held out one of the stones and took a few slow steps forward.

Midian looked at her, and her eyes widened in shock. "You are still alive?"

157

"For now. Why?"

"Eadric killed her mate. Revenge was mandated."

"Why now?"

Midian smirked. "We needed to get past his defenses. You handed us the spell. We had to strike today because of your exam."

Imara nodded slightly in understanding. "I was leaving the school."

"This was our chance. So, how will you spend your last few minutes?"

Imara gave her a cold smile. "You won't need to know that."

She held out the hand with the stone in it, and with some concentration and a few murmured words, she ripped Midian's spectre from her and put it in the pebble.

Midian gasped, twitched, and her serpent body faded, leaving only her human form behind.

"What... what did you do?"

Imara looked at her in surprise. "You and your sister took mage courses, became masters. I took your magic from you and put it in this pebble. It will explode in a few seconds, but enjoy being human for the rest of your natural, human lifespan."

She looked to Luken. "Please throw the pebble as hard as you can."

Michael grabbed it and hurled it upward. "Luken doesn't have a good pitching arm."

The stone shattered in the air above them in a cloud of bright blue particles.

The scream that heralded the approach of the other lamia was all that Imara needed. She turned and pulled on the magic as hard as she could, breaking the woman free of her shifted body as centuries of magic were crammed into the small rock. She threw the stone upward, and it was still too close when it exploded.

Arms came around her and lifted her up; she heard voices calling her name, but everything around her was dark. At least her family was safe.

She woke several times with lights flaring around her and folk shouting orders. Each time she sought the comfort of Mr. E, he whispered in her thoughts. *Still here, Imara. You lie quiet and let them help you.*

You are pushy for a kitten. I am glad you are all right.

You made sure of that. It was an amazing spell; now, go to sleep and let them heal you.

Bossy kitty.

You bet I am.

She smiled and stopped fighting sleep.

Waking up in a pristine white tent was a surprise. She thought she had been treated at the college medical centre.

The mage from earlier was sitting at her bedside. He was older, had a thick wave of black hair that caressed the back edge of his collar with the rest combed back, a small silver streak was just starting over one temple. His face was slightly dusky with a long, straight nose that was nearly a weapon in itself but managed to make his face—as a whole—rather handsome. The amber eyes made her pause. She knew those eyes.

"Who are you?" Her first words were a little rude, but she meant them.

"My dearest mage, I am amazed you don't recognize me in this form."

She stared at him and blinked. "Mr. E?"

"Please, when I look like this, call me Eadric."

She blinked again. She went to rub her eyes, but an IV confined her hand.

She looked up and found a red bag hanging from a pole. "What?"

"Ah, the lamia venom had completely infiltrated your systems, so several complete transfusions were necessary. Your mother was not a match, nor was Luken, oddly enough. Michael and Alexander were matches, as were Lio, Hyl, Kitigan, and several other students who saw your fight and volunteered to be type tested."

She blushed. "They all donated?"

"There was a line of XIA agents being tested. Several of them donated, and their blood was the first rinse to get the venom out of your system. Magic has been used to keep you stable, but everyone was relieved when you began to breathe on your own again."

He reached out and squeezed her free hand.

"So, you are a person now?"

He cocked his head. "I am still your familiar, but you gave me what I needed to fight for our lives. So, now, I have a few more forms. This one included."

She scowled. "Was that what you looked like?"

"It is fairly close. I was older when I was captured, but I think that the small silver streak is a nice touch." He lifted his head, and she burst out into sobs.

He sighed and got up, carefully lifting her out of the bed and setting her on his lap with the IV next to them.

When she finished crying, he whispered, "This is a turn of events, huh? Normally I am in your lap."

She snickered and leaned against his shoulder. "Are you safe now?"

"As safe as I can be. The pardon has come through from the guild, by the way. You are my last mage."

She gasped and looked up. "Wonderful. How do I set you lose?"

"Oh, I am not getting loose, not until you get a familiar to replace me that is as

163

magnificent as I am. You also have a lot of plans for the future, and I am in them, so it would be rude to have to adjust your trajectory."

She laughed. "Right. Thank you. Are you still a kitten?"

"I can choose the kitten for easy transport, a larger cat when I am on my own, or my hellcat appearance if need be."

"Wow. That must be nice."

He gave her a gentle hug. "It truly is. How are you going to adapt to the scars?"

Imara looked down at the silvery slices that crossed her arm in places, and she shrugged. "I will adapt. They are part of me now, and I don't recall reading about a lot of lamia survivors."

"There are none. They die screaming within a day of their attack. You got lucky that you were close enough to call for help."

She smiled. "I called for Reegar. He would know what I wanted. Where is he, by the way?"

"He's waiting outside with the others. We didn't want to overwhelm you."

The air ruffled the walls of the tent. "Where are we, by the way?"

"Ritual Space. Adrea offered to host your transfusions and recuperation here so that no one could interfere with it."

She wrinkled her nose. "Did you play tag with Blueberry?"

"Of course. He is an excellent companion and wonderful conversationalist. You have introduced me to the most fascinating people." He grinned and gave her another hug.

She sighed and carefully got to her feet, holding the IV pole in one hand. She walked slowly with the soft white gown clinging tightly to her in an ancient toga design. She opened the tent flap and walked out into afternoon sun.

Mr. E was behind her and taller than she would have imagined.

A gathering of people was sitting in another marquee, so Imara wandered over to where her friends, family, and intimidating strangers were gathered.

Bara was sitting and holding Luken's hand, or she was holding his.

Imara walked up to her, and she asked the most important question of all. "Was there any of that cake left over? I am pretty sure I passed the exam."

Luken whooped and jumped up, hugging her tight before letting Bara in for her turn.

The next twenty minutes were rounds of tears, hugs, and a sweet kiss from Argus that made her rise up on her toes.

"I didn't know if you would make it." He whispered it against her ear.

"I didn't either."

"I don't want to lose you."

She leaned back and smiled at him. "I

will always fight to stay."

"I will have to take that as good enough."

"You will. Just as I have to take your little journeys into homicide and raging trolls as part and parcel of who you are. You have your world, and I am glad it crossed into mine." She stroked his cheek.

Chancellor Mirrin cleared her throat. "Should I be giving some kind of safe-sex speech here?"

Reegar laughed. "It wouldn't do any good. Imara will take care of herself, or she will choose not to. You have little say in the matter. She's a strong person."

Imara hugged Argus and looked at Reegar. "You are still able to roam?"

"Yes, whatever you did went into the bedrock of the college. All of the spectres have a range they hadn't imagined, though only I retain the physical presence."

"You are special."

He grinned and then sobered. "That was dangerous."

"Detonating the spell on my body? Yeah."

"No, facing a lamia."

"Oh, that wasn't a choice. We finished confirming the exam, and then, she shook my hand, and the first venom entered my system. I didn't do anything after that but run as long as I could. I think I made it thirty feet outside the lab before N'sha got me."

Reegar blinked. "Then what happened?"

"I couldn't reach Mr. E, so I called the spectres. You were the only one that showed up, but I know that you knew about the bracelet. If they were after my familiar, all I could do was give him the tools to help himself. I had no idea anyone else would show up."

Argus murmured, "Luken called me."

Mirrin nodded, "And me."

Imara reached out, and Luken came to let her squeeze his hand. "Thank you. I may be pretty flippant about it, but I like being alive."

He grinned. "It was my pleasure. I am just glad that I guessed Argus's number on the first try."

The folks gathered laughed at what they thought was a joke, but Imara looked at Luken and knew the truth. He had simply gotten lucky. It was what he did.

Chapter Eleven

$\mathcal{I}$t had been two weeks since she left Ritual Space and returned to the college. Paperwork had become part of everyday life. She had to make out incident reports for the Mage Guild, the XIA, and the Death Keepers. Her manoeuvre of pulling the spectres out of living lamia had caused a lot of fuss.

If it weren't for her injuries, every single one of those governing bodies would have arrested her, but as it was, she simply got a lecture on not doing it again.

Reegar and his lover were off on holiday for a few days, which disappointed Imara. She was about to leave the Hall, and he wasn't even home.

Bara and Luken were on their way to a movie, and Mr. E was engaged in the most disturbing development of all. He was dating her mother.

So that was how Imara found herself free of paperwork with no friends available and Argus over an hour away.

"I guess I could watch a movie." She sat on the couch and turned on the television. Spare time was not something she had had in the last decade.

Her paperwork for a commercial magic license should be confirmed any day now, and then, she needed to make the move to Redbird City.

Imara stared blankly at the screen while she checked off all the boxes for her new occupation. The estate agent had hired a cleaner to go through the rooms and tidy up, a basic bedroom suite and kitchen appliances had been set up upstairs from her offices, and her would-be home was ready.

A tribunal had confirmed that she had passed her course at master's level, and when she knew she had done her best, she had made sure that Carlos was tested on his work as well.

Once she had the license, she would be able to open up a website and wait for clients. She always had the Death Keeper guild for a basic income, but she wanted her own clients.

Her mind went from hopeful to dark in an instant, and she remembered pulling the spectres from the lamias. She stared at her hands, and she shook at the energy that she had been holding in the palm of her hands. She had pulled centuries of magic away from its owners as if they had no true attachment to it. That was terrifying.

She was lost in thought when a pinging rang out. She lifted her head and listened. *Ping.*

Imara got to her feet and walked toward the sound, realizing that it was coming from her room.

She carefully walked into her space, and the doorway to Ritual Space was open and glowing. There was only one person who could open it, so Imara put on some shoes and stepped through, ready to do battle with Adrea's enemies.

"Surprise!" The roar of voices shocked the hell out of Imara, and she fell on her ass the moment that the sound hit her.

Argus came to her rescue and helped her to her feet. There was a huge banner levitating in the air and the words, *Congratulations, Imara* hovered above the crowd.

She looked up at him. "What the hell?"

Reegar and Lee were standing together and smiling. Lee murmured, "You are underdressed. This is a black-tie affair."

A wave of his hand later and she was wearing one of the gowns that Bara had designed for her. Her running shoes were still intact, and that made Imara smile.

Argus offered her his arm, and she took it, walking through the crowd and greeting all the people who came to celebrate something.

"Why are we here?" Imara murmured it.

"Your commercial magic license came in today. Reegar and your mother hid it so that we could still have the graduation party. Everyone here has been part of your journey and part of your fight. That group of XIA officers there offered their blood for you, without knowing you. They only knew of your character via other agents and that was enough to bring them out when they thought they could help."

"They are running through my veins

right now." She smiled at them, and they raised cups to her.

"Yes, but I just wanted you to see how many people are excited to see you reach your goals. We all are. You have a community."

She leaned against him and whispered. "I know. The moment that I woke up in the tent, I knew that it had taken tremendous effort to get me back."

"I wish I had been able to help."

"You kept her from slicing me to pieces. That was huge."

"I meant in your recovery."

She laughed. "Of course, you disregard the action and putting your life in danger."

"That is what I do. Your mother wields a wicked lightning blast, by the way."

"Glad to hear it. I didn't know that she was weather trained."

"I think that this is the moment when

you can start to learn about your life or, at least, your family before you were born."

Mirrin, with her arm linked with Mr. E's, came toward her. "Imara, please come this way. I have some folk I would like you to meet."

"Certainly. Mother, can you stop cuddling up to my cat?"

Mirrin grinned. "No. You will get used to it. Eadric is charming, caring, and he loves you as much as I do. It is normal for us to be together."

Imara linked arms with her mother and eased her away from a smug Mr. E. "Fine. But if you give me a new brother or sister, expect hairballs."

Mirrin gave a glorious and bright laugh as she and Imara headed to a group of people who were enjoying the beverages and snacks at the party.

"Imara, this is your grandmother and grandfather, Ida and Hector. These are some of your cousins and their children. This is one chunk of the Deepford-Smythe family."

"I am pleased to meet you." She looked around and saw a number of familiar faces. Casually, throughout her life, she had met each person at the table. "I know you."

Ida smiled. "We know you. We have made every effort to meet you and support you across your life. It is a deep relief that you made it this far and are now a Master Mage."

Imara nodded and smiled. "I remember. I remember you all."

One cousin had bought cookies from her at a school bake sale, another had helped her change a flat tire, another picked up her wallet and returned it to her in the store. Her grandparents had been at her first job while she was learning how to energize the spectres.

"You have watched me."

177

Ida smiled and shook her head. "Oh no. No legally. The Demiels were very strict on your exposure to our side of the family. Legally, we were not allowed to let you know you had any family. By the way, we are having a gathering at the end of next month in Redbird City. You are welcome to attend if you like."

Mirrin gave her a hug. "She might be overwhelmed. I will get her the information and location."

Imara smiled. "I will look into it. I am about to open my own business, so my schedule is currently unknown."

Ida nodded. "I understand. We will keep issuing the invitations, so when you are ready, we will be there."

It was the best thing she could have said. "Thank you."

Ida inclined her head. "We are so proud of what you have done on your own, and we look forward to meeting you properly, but for today, enjoy your party. You have more than earned it."

Mirrin nodded. "They are not wrong."

Imara looked around to see Benny flapping her hands, and so, she excused herself and went to meet Benny to be formally introduced to her parents.

It was part of being the guest of the hour, so Imara went along and met and greeted folk who had been involved in her survival and—in some cases—existence. It was a relief when she could creep away to a corner and simply get her head together.

She was sitting at the table when a lithe black cat jumped up and sat in front of her. She smiled. "You are exceptionally dramatic as a proper cat."

He inclined his head. *Thank you. Are you overwhelmed?*

"Yes. Before I got here, I was alone in the universe with one friend. Now, I am bonded to you, and everybody here has some kind of stake in my life. I know them, they know me, and we like each other. This is... not what I was preparing for."

He shifted into his mage form. "I know. I am in your mind, and you are in mine. I know that simply opening yourself up to me was huge. This is overwhelming."

"A little. I am happy about it. So very happy about it."

"I can feel that, too."

She grinned. "You know what I can't get over?"

"What?"

She swatted him on the arm. "My kitten is dating my mom!"

He laughed out loud. "It has been a while for both of us, and we have you in common, so what harm is there?"

Imara grabbed the front of his mage robes and pulled him in. "Stop slipping the privacy wall between us when you and she are making out. It is not a way to keep me sane."

His cheeks blushed, and a moment later, her little kitten was looking up at her, and he let out a little *mew*.

"Oh, you are a manipulative little guy." She picked him up and cuddled him, scratching behind his ears.

The party was in full swing. Her family was talking, the XIA were arm wrestling, her friends were eating blunderberries and trying to figure out what they were tasting, so Imara got up and carried Mr. E along to try and shed some clarity on the flavour.

A white and blue streak went past her feet, and Mr. E was in the air in the next minute, booting through the crowd and trying to catch the bunny alpha of Ritual Space.

She giggled and walked over to the most formal berry tasting she had ever been a part of.

Imara made coffee the next morning for the survivors of the party who had made it back to Reegar Hall.

Mr. E was asleep in a pie pan that was coated with purple berry juice, Reegar and Lee were cuddled up on a couch. Bara was sleeping sitting up, and Luken was head down on the table. Kitigan was curled up in the library. Mirrin was curled up in a ball on the love seat.

Imara looked at the friends and family around her and doubled the coffee shot. They were going to need it. That had been a ton of blunderberry pie.

She picked Mr. E up, and the pie pan came with him. When he moved his paws, the pan released and hit the table with a clatter.

No one even moved.

She grinned and went to wash off her kitten, glancing at her bracelet and smiling again. "Well, it seems that I am all alone once again."

My eyes are sticky.

"You are getting a bath. You are suffering from blunderberry hangover, just like everyone else."

Why aren't you sleepy? You ate three times as much as Kitty did.

"I know. I guess I just got lucky. What are the odds of that." She grinned as he gave her a silent groan, and as she scrubbed the purple juice from her familiar, she realized that that was exactly what had happened.

The lamia had followed her in a projected form, which accounted for the two extra spectres the day she took the mage guides around the memorial garden. If she had used the fading garden, she would have summoned them into the memorial area, she would have been dead on the spot. Forcing them to hunt her in the open had made them rework their attack, and that had let her get to the point where Imara could summon

183

the help she needed. It had just been luck, instinct, and timing.

With a clean and scrawny familiar, she rubbed him with a fluffy towel until he looked more like a kitten and less like a rat then carried him back downstairs where she was making breakfast for ten. Her studies were done, she had her license, it was now time to get ready to leave the safety of Reegar Hall and step into the world.

She looked at the unconscious friends and family as she made bacon and pancakes. The difference in this move to Redbird City was that she wasn't going to be alone. It was going to take effort to get her grin off her face.

Epilogue

The door needed a slight nudge to get it open, but it opened. Imara looked down at Mr. E, and she nodded. "This is it."

He gave her a polite but attentive gaze from his new height. "It looks to be in good condition."

She grinned. "This is just the exterior door, but I like your enthusiasm."

Imara pushed the door open all the way, and the slightly dry odour of a closed building met her senses. It was mixed with the scent of newly sawn wood, and that scent confused her.

"Who the heck has been doing work here?" Imara let Mr. E in and closed the door behind her newly reshaped familiar.

Mr. E didn't respond, but there was a swish to his tail that said he was up to something. The dark, polished wood of the hall led to the right and left. She wanted to make the left into her office and the right into a conference room. Her application for a building permit was with all of her belongings out in the car.

Her beloved kitty and favourite buddy was heading straight for the office space.

She moved carefully around the corner, and she paused in shock when she saw the sketch from her file in full detail in the space. Everything from the desk, filing cabinets, bookshelves, ritual area, and coffee machine in the corner, were all exactly as she had doodled them.

Mr. E hopped up onto his supervisory stand, and he watched her.

She felt the tears starting to run down

her cheeks. Over a decade of planning
and here was her office. She had her
space, it was paid for, her license to en-
gage in public magic had come through,
and she was a Master Death Keeper and
had full membership in the Mage Guild.

She sniffled and wiped the tears from
her cheeks. "Right. Well, now, I just
need the signage and advertising, and
we will literally be in business."

He lifted and licked one of his paws.
You might want to check outside.

Imara turned toward the door, and
then, she heard a scrape. There was a
whir, and she walked down the entry
hallway to the front door, opening it
slowly. A cluster of shadows was on the
sidewalk, but it was a familiar cluster.

She closed the door, but a scent
caught her again. She looked at the door,
and it read, *Spectral Consulting, I. Mirrin, Master Death Keeper, Commercial
Master Mage.*

When she turned back to the folks who were installing the hanging sign-board nine feet over the sidewalk, she grinned at the very decorous but precise signage. The small spectral stone embedded in a corner of the sign gave it the touch that it needed to catch attention.

When the installation crew was done, she smiled as they pulled off their concealing head wraps. Argus smiled ruefully. "We wanted to get it done before you came back out."

She walked up to him and wrapped her arms around him. "I was happy-crying inside, and it freaked Mr. E out, so he decided I needed a distraction. This is amazing. Thank you!"

He held her close, and he sighed happily, as he always did when she cuddled up to him.

Freddy snickered. "You two look so wrong."

Imara looked around Argus, and she

grinned. "I know. I am too mature for him, but his age makes up for it."

Freddy chuckled. "I thought that he was energy and life, and you were death, but I suppose your description could be right. You are serious, and he... isn't."

Argus turned to look at Freddy over his shoulder. "I am very serious when it comes to Imara."

The woman grinned, and she looked up. "Well, what do you think, Spectral Consultant?"

Imara leaned back and took in the display. Bara and Luken were standing near the back of the pack, Argus's XIA team was grinning at her, and one of them was still wearing Freddy as an epaulet.

"I think that this is just the way I wanted to see my business start. In the dark with friends being weird and dressing like ninjas."

They looked at her, themselves, and

then giggles broke up their serious gathering.

"So, who wants to help me break in the coffeemaker?" Imara laughed.

Freddy winked. "I am more a fan of breaking into the mini bar."

Imara stared. "I have one of those?"

"You have two. Now, you just have to find them." Freddy linked her arm with Imara and hauled her toward the door. Imara looked back over her shoulder, and everyone was slowly trickling toward them.

It was time to get the party started.

Imara sat on her boardroom table and watched the XIA officers smash a piñata with stress balls. Mr. E was the scorekeeper. He chased the balls that rolled under the furniture.

Freddy produced a laptop, and she sat next to Imara. "This was my gift for you."

To Imara's shock, her business had a
website, and there were already eighty-
five hits and two messages waiting for
her.

"When did you do this?"

"I pulled it together with a little help
from Argus. It turns out that I am pretty
good at web design when I choose to be.
See, it even has a calendar so you can
black out dates when you need to."

"It doesn't tell folks where I will be,
does it?"

"No. It just says that you are unavail-
able for bookings or consultations."

Imara followed her instructions and
got into the messages. To her shock,
both were genuine inquiries for her services. "Wow. They are asking about my
fees."

"So? The Death Keeper guild had its
own fee structure. This is no different.
In fact, you can charge more as you have
all the credentials and a service that no

one on this side of the continent can offer."

Imara blinked slowly. "Right. I keep forgetting about that."

Mr. E bounded up from under the couch with one of the projectiles in his jaws. She knew he was a man in a cat form, but he looked for all the world like a proud hunter.

You are definitely one of a kind, Imara Mirrin Deepford-Smythe Demiel. He set the stress ball down next to her hand. *If the hellhound can help you manage your business efforts, enjoy the assistance. It will give me a break.*

She smiled and stroked his head. "I am taking any help that is offered."

Freddy looked at her and grinned, going into depth on how to manage the website.

When Imara glanced down at Mr. E, he batted the toy with his paw, and it struck the piñata, splitting the pixie wide open and scattering candy everywhere.

The men hooted and dove for it while Imara rubbed Mr. E's head. "Nice shot."

You should see me with opposable thumbs.

She chuckled. "I have. Did you have to hit on my mom?"

Chancellor Mirrin is an attractive woman and nowhere near her prime. We have a date next weekend.

Imara grinned. "Do you?"

Yes, as do you. If Argus gets out of hand, I am only a thought away, but I believe you two would benefit from a lack of my attention.

Argus was crouched over and picking candy carefully from the pile. He walked over to her, kissed her lightly and placed the candy in her hands. It was all her favourites.

"Happy business warming."

She looked up at him in bemusement and whispered, "Thank you."

Freddy looked at them both, and she eased away.

Argus took the spot that had been occupied by the hellhound, and he whispered, "Are you happy with how things have worked out?"

She smiled. "This is the start of something new, exciting and terrifying. I am delighted with how it turned out."

He frowned. "Even the threats to your life?"

"They brought me into contact with people I never would have met. I would not have spoken to you if the teacher hadn't been such a creep. Once I met you, I was able to help the XIA member possessed by a spectre—"

"Put yourself in the path of a serial killer."

"I made every course with honours."

"And only had to commit a few breaking and entering as well as magical ingress crimes."

She leaned against him. "But those events led me to new friends and learning about what I was capable of. I am so much stronger now that I know who I am and what my family is actually like, which helps me know myself a little better."

"Even if half of them are jerks?"

"Especially because of that. I know that it is in me now, and I can be on guard for it."

He shook his head in astonishment.

"You have the most peculiarly upbeat attitude. It is one of the things that I treasure about you."

She smiled. "I know. It is the hardest thing to maintain, but the most rewarding in the long run."

He chuckled, and she settled against him, watching the rest of the party come up with a new game involving empty and not empty beverage cups on heads, targets for the spongy stress balls. Mr. E was curled up against her other hip, and she was warm and secure for this first night in her new business with her apartment just above it.

Tonight, was the first night of her business, and it marked the start of her actual courtship with Argus. A lot of firsts were taking place in the next few weeks, and Imara could hardly wait to get to them.

At this point, Imara officially joins the plotline of An Obscure Magic. She is going to play a part in the lives of the other characters, and perhaps Mr. E will continue his bizarre flirtation with her mother. I never suspected that Mirrin was a cat lady, but Mr. E knew it all along.

Author's Note

Imara will appear in *Hellhound in a Handbag*. Freddy's story. Finally.

This series has been an effort to embed Imara and Mr. E in the Obscure Magic universe. I think I accomplished that goal.

The real Mr. E likes when I write his alter ego. He gets more head scratchies that way.

Thanks for reading,

Viola Grace

About the Author

Viola Grace (aka Zenina Masters) is a Canadian sci-fi/paranormal romance writer with ambitions to keep writing for the rest of her life. She specializes in short stories because the thrill of discovery, of all those firsts, is what keeps her writing.

An artist who enjoys a story that catches you up, whirls you around and sets you down with a smile on your face is all she endeavours to be. She prefers to leave the drama to those who are better suited to it, she always goes for the cheap laugh.